Jason's
Money Tree

Original title: Jason and the Money Tree

by **SONIA LEVITIN**

Illustrated by Pat Grant Porter

Cover by Dan Dickus

SCHOLASTIC BOOK SERVICES
NEW YORK · TORONTO · LONDON · AUCKLAND · SYDNEY · TOKYO

For Danny and Shari, with love

ISBN: 0-590-01586-9

Text copyright © 1974 by Sonia Levitin. Illustrations copyright © 1974 by Harcourt Brace Jovanovich, Inc. This edition is published by Scholastic Book Services, a division of Scholastic Magazines, Inc., by arrangement with Harcourt Brace Jovanovich, Inc.

13 12 11 10 9 8 7 6 5 4 3   0 1 2 3/8

Contents

The Strange Gift

"Jason Galloway," he told himself sternly and in amazement, "you've really flipped!"

For a sensible boy of eleven (going on twelve, nearly *thirteen!*) to have such an idea was downright crazy. A money tree! No, never in a million years could money grow on a tree. Never!

But — but signs kept pointing all in the same direction, suggesting, hinting, telling him that something extraordinary was about to happen.

How had it begun? Jason sat on his bed, frowning, his head propped in his hands. Before him lay the evidence. The crumpled fortune from a fortune cookie read, "Your efforts will soon bear fruit." There, too, lay the gifts Grandpa had left him, the ivory ball, the

1

gold pocket watch, and the mysterious ten-dollar bill.

Not present, but vivid in his mind, were the two most significant clues: his dream last night and the rainbow late this afternoon. Everything pointed to only one possible conclusion — something was about to happen, something magical. And although Jason was a reasonable, sensible boy who didn't believe a bit in magic, three words kept ringing and singing through his mind. The money tree. The money tree.

For hours now, his sensible self had argued against the nutty idea that it could happen. The nutty idea was slowly but steadily winning out.

Ever since Grandpa had died, leaving him the silver box with these three gifts inside, Jason had been searching for a meaning. He understood why Grandpa had left him the ivory ball. It was really many balls, one inside the other. Each was carved with a different design. Years ago, when Grandpa had told him it was made from a single piece of ivory, Jason had exclaimed, "That's impossible!"

"Nothing is impossible," Grandpa had insisted, "and here's the proof."

Yes, the ivory ball had a meaning. It was Grandpa's way of making him remember, "Nothing is impossible!" And the watch, too, was special. It had belonged to Grandpa's father, and now it seemed to throb in Jason's hand.

"Patience!" Grandpa used to say, fingering the watch. "Time will explain it all."

But Jason could find no explanation for the third gift, a soiled and crumpled ten-dollar bill. Why, Grandpa had never paid much attention to money, and he seldom had more than a dollar in his pocket. Grandpa would never have left him an ordinary old ten-dollar bill — unless it had a meaning.

Strangely, whenever Jason started to spend it, something seemed to pull him back. "Don't do it!" a voice inside him would cry. "You'll be sorry. Think — what would Grandpa want you to do with this ten-dollar bill?"

But though Jason had pondered the problem for weeks, no solution appeared. Then yesterday he'd begun to remember things Grandpa had said. The sayings seemed unrelated at first. Then they began to fit together.

"With time and a little patience," Grandpa used to say, "you can make anything grow."

Time, patience, growing things — it began to add up. Then, at supper last night, Jason had picked the cookie with this fortune: "Your efforts will soon bear fruit."

Obviously, a person had to plant something for it to bear fruit. And what could he plant? What fine fruit could possibly grow here in foggy, dingy Silverview?

"With time and a little patience and a touch of magic in your fingers..." Yes, Grandpa had had a certain magic in his fingers, a green thumb, a way with growing things. His rubber plant had grown so tall that people mistook it for a banana tree. Orchids and camellias had streamed out of flowerpots on Grandpa's windowsill. And on Grandpa's balcony in San Francisco, where it was seldom really warm, Grandpa had grown a sturdy little lemon tree. From it he used to pick fresh lemons for his salad, declaring with a smile, "You see, nothing is impossible."

Last night Jason had felt the same strange feeling he'd felt the night before Dinah was born, heavy expectation and great certainty. Something was about to happen, now! Then came the marvelous dream.

"Of course," Jason told himself, "dreams are only the fulfillment of your wishes." And he did wish for many things — more time with Dad, a house in the country, and money. Oh, yes, he could do with a bit more money!

In his dream Jason had planted Grandpa's ten-dollar bill. Grandpa stood by, murmuring, "With time and a little patience you can make anything grow."

Overhead, an airplane poured out white-chalk letters against the black sky, "YOUR EFFORTS WILL SOON BEAR FRUIT."

In his dream the ten-dollar bill had sprouted and grown into a beautiful money tree, filled with ten-dollar bills.

This was no ordinary dream. All day Jason sensed its promise, its almost supernatural power. It filled him with delight, so that he didn't mind doing his chores. He didn't mind having to be quiet so Dad could study. He didn't even mind the rain.

At dusk the rain stopped, and from his bedroom window Jason saw a rainbow. Never, never had he seen one like it. It began far beyond the ocean cliffs at the edge of Silverview. It rose across the sky, a wide band of flowing colors. It arched over all the identical little square houses with their identical gray-shingled roofs. And it ended in Jason's backyard.

Clearly, if ever there was an omen, a sign from somewhere beyond, this was it.

Although he was quite alone, Jason couldn't help feeling a little embarrassed as he tiptoed out into the backyard with the ten-dollar bill in his pocket. The sky was astonishingly clear for Silverview. The moon hung like a round face, with a streak of cloud across it, curved upward like a smile.

"Go ahead!" it seemed to say slyly. "What have you got to lose?"

If he failed, nobody would ever know. His parents and baby Dinah were fast asleep. And they never came out into the backyard anyway. It was too cold and dismal. Only Jason came here, for privacy or to mow the stubby patch of lawn occasionally.

Still Jason hesitated. It was just too absurd! From next door came the faint sound of the Quinley's TV set. But underneath it he heard a strange buzzing. It surrounded him, urged him. "Hurry! Go on. Try it."

The urgent buzzing made him search the sky. Suddenly a lone sea gull passed under the moon, dipping its wing. With a loud squawk it seemed to say, "Get on with it! We both know what you're here for."

Jason swallowed hard, then sighed deeply. All right. He would go through the motions anyway. What's wrong with letting yourself almost believe, just for once, that magic can happen?

"I'm just pretending," he told himself as he took up the flowerpot from beside the fence. "I'm pretending because I need a little excitement in my life. I'm tired of being quiet and lonesome, of waiting and making plans that never amount to anything."

With an old trowel he scraped up a mound of sandy soil and filled the flowerpot. Then he laid the ten-dollar bill on top. The money shimmered in the moonlight. Now the silence was complete. Something more was obviously expected of him. An incantation, perhaps? What magic words would make money grow?

Jason cleared his throat, threw back his head, and whispered as loudly as he dared:

"In the moonlight hush
By the ink-black bush..."

He groaned. Poetry was definitely not his talent. He tried again.

"In the moonlight beams
Where the sea gull screams..."

Jason decided to skip incantations. Why would he need one? If you've got the magic touch, that's all you need. He scooped up another trowelful of soil, covered over the ten-dollar bill, and gave it several pats.

As he patted the soil, a tremendous feeling of power and certainty came over him. He could feel it vibrating through his body like a sonic boom, tingling down into his fingers. "Yes!" he thought, breathing heavily. "Nothing is impossible!" He stretched out his arms, as if to embrace all the supernatural forces gathered here in the moonlight. "Yes," he whispered, "I believe! When all the circumstances are exactly right, magic can be made by ordinary people like me."

He quickly put the flowerpot back beside the fence. Feverishly warm now, he recalled all the magical mysteries he had ever heard. In Arizona a cool spring had suddenly bubbled up out of the desert. Flying saucers were spotted in Colorado. In a house in Ohio, pictures started falling off the walls, and dishes sailed across the rooms and hit people on the head. According to the newspaper, even scientists were baffled. At last a famous university professor had concluded that it must be a poltergeist. A ghost! A mischievous ghost who got his kicks playing pranks and throwing dishes! It was absolutely illogical. But if a professor could believe in a poltergeist, then he, Jason Galloway, could believe in a money tree.

Joyously, Jason ran back to the house. He had never felt so excited, so in tune with everything in the world. He did have a special talent, inherited from Grandpa, a knack for making things grow. And somehow fate had chosen him to bring about the impossible.

At last Jason lay in his bed, worn out by the frenzy of his thoughts. His breathing was calm again, his body limp. Gone was the excitement. Coldly, he told himself, "Jason Galloway, you've really flipped. Money doesn't grow on trees. First thing in the morning, you'd better go dig up that ten-dollar bill."

He closed his eyes, became himself again. First thing in the morning, he decided, he'd go and dig it up. And that would be the end of that.

The Sprout

In the morning Jason's mother came to wake him. "Hey, get up lazybones!" She shook him gently. "Have you forgotten about your job?" By her smile Jason could see how proud she was.

Jason scrubbed his face, slicked down his hair, and grinned at himself in the mirror. It wasn't easy for a boy his age to get a summer job, even part-time. Jason had not only landed this job — he had created it.

Mr. Matroni ran the smallest store in Silverview Shopping Center. The narrow little shop was wedged into a corner between the supermarket and the bright, modern drugstore.

From the day Mr. Matroni had opened the shop,

Jason had been a steady browser. Mom was unimpressed. "What an odd assortment of things," she said. "Records, sporting equipment, models — none of them really go together."

"They're all things kids like," Jason told her. "That's how they go together. Mr. Matroni's even thinking of putting in a candy counter."

"Where would he put it? On the ceiling?"

"Maybe," Jason said with a grin. "Mr. Matroni understands kids. He lets them come in and listen to records in the little booth for as long as they want."

"I should think some of them would take advantage of that privilege," Mom had said. "I don't see how he can handle all those kids by himself."

That was how Jason got his idea. It didn't take a lot of brains to see that the kids were driving Mr. Matroni right out of his mind. Teen-agers made Matroni's their meeting place. Little boys poked through the boxes of airplane models and got the pieces all mixed up. Boys came in and tested out the baseballs. Fortunately, Jason happened to be there when several records were smashed by a high fly.

Mr. Matroni looked desperate. He tugged at his hair until it stood out like thistles.

Jason walked over to him and said, "Somebody ought to keep those kids in line."

Mr. Matroni sighed and rolled his eyes. "I can't take it much longer," he admitted. "My little store is turning into a three-ring circus."

"You need help," Jason said. "Couldn't your wife come and help you?"

"Impossible. My home is an even bigger three-ring circus than my store." Turning aside, he called, "Little boy, *please* don't chew on that baseball bat." He nodded to Jason. "Just like my youngest — she chews on chair legs. I've got four kids, two still in diapers."

"I know what you mean," Jason replied sympathetically. "My baby sister is still in diapers, and she just started to walk. She gets into everything, and if we don't watch her, she dumps things in the toilet."

"Just like my firstborn." Mr. Matroni nodded in agreement.

Jason squatted down to help Mr. Matroni with the broken records. Then he stood up tall as he could. "Mr. Matroni," he said, "I'd like to work for you."

"Jason, I think you are too young."

"I'm eleven, going on twelve — almost *thirteen!*" Jason replied, raising his head. He was nearly as tall as Mr. Matroni.

"No, thank you."

"I've had experience in handling kids."

"No. I'm sorry."

"Mr. Matroni," said Jason, "I'd work without pay."

Mr. Matroni froze, dropped the broken records

"Without pay," Jason repeated. "I need the expe-

rience. Six years from now I'll be going to college. I might have to work my way through. You can never get a job without experience. But how do you get that first job in the first place? Without pay," Jason said.

"Jason," said Mr. Matroni, "you are a reasonable boy."

"I could come in every Saturday," Jason suggested.

"Saturdays are murder," Mr. Matroni said. "What I really need is someone to..." His gaze swept over the untidy shelves, the unkempt teen-agers, the unruly little boys.

"Someone to keep an eye on things," Jason said smoothly. "I'd straighten up the shelves. I'd watch the little kids and help them decide what they want."

"And you could put on the records for the teen-agers," Mr. Matroni added, beaming. "I can't let everybody fool around with that phonograph. It's already broken down twice."

"And I know all the latest hits," Jason added. "I'll know just what they mean when they ask for them."

"Jason, you are saving my life. One girl came in and asked for the *Jefferson Airplane*. I spent half an hour looking for it in the model catalogue before she told me it was the name of a singing group."

Jason stifled a giggle. Mr. Matroni thrust out his hand, and with a broad smile he exclaimed, "Shake, partner!"

"Partner!" The triumph of it sent Jason speeding

down the street like a track star, brought him roaring in the front door, shouting, "I've got a job with Mr. Matroni!"

Dad peered up from his law books. "Child labor," he said, "is against the law."

Jason was stunned.

"Jonathan!" Mom said sternly, glaring at Dad.

"I'll be glad to examine your contract," Dad continued, "for a slight fee, of course."

"Jonathan!" Mom said warningly.

"I don't have a contract," Jason said. "But we shook hands."

"Ah. And may I ask about your salary?"

"No money," Jason said. "We're friends."

Suddenly Dad broke into a grin and clasped Jason's shoulder. "I'm proud of you, son. There is definitely no law against friendship."

Then Dad reached into his pocket. "Every day that you work for Mr. Matroni," he said, "I'll give you fifty cents for refreshments. I suppose it would seem undignified to bring your lunch in a paper bag."

For the past six Saturdays Jason had worked for Mr. Matroni. By the end of the day he was so tired that he was almost seeing double. But it was a good, satisfied kind of tiredness. And last week Mr. Matroni had brought out a freshly laundered blue smock. It was exactly like the one Mr. Matroni wore, except that the name *Jason* was stitched in red letters over the pocket.

"I figured you'd need this," said Mr. Matroni, "to protect your clothing. It gets dusty in here."

The smock gave Jason more than money. It gave him dignity. Even the teen-agers looked at him with new respect, and kids in the neighborhood stopped him on the street to say admiringly, "Hey, you work at Matroni's, don't you?"

Now, as Jason ran out the door and down the street, he nearly bumped into Dave Parker, who was loading fishing gear into the car. "Guess what?" Dave called out. "I'm gonna try out my new pole!"

"Gee, that's great." Jason gazed at the pole, trying to conceal his sudden longing. Mr. Parker came out carrying a camp stove.

"Hi there, Jason," he said, and for an instant their eyes met. Mr. Parker's pitying look swept away all Jason's pride and dignity. "Poor kid," it said. "Poor kid has to work while we go fishing."

All day at the store, Mr. Parker's look nagged at Jason. His vague longing grew into an overwhelming desire not only for a fishing pole, but for all the tempting wares that surrounded him. Pocket-sized transistor radios, gleaming tackle boxes, clean white baseballs and mitts that smelled strongly of new leather — oh, how he wanted them all!

Suddenly, Jason remembered the ten-dollar bill in the flowerpot. He simply had to spend it!

So great was Jason's desire to get home that at four o'clock, when the afternoon rush was over,

Jason said to Mr. Matroni, "I guess you won't need me anymore today."

"Sure, go ahead." Then Mr. Matroni rang up the "No Sale" key on the cash register. "Jason," he said, "you understand that I can't afford to pay you. But" — he dipped his hand into the register and brought out a dollar — "every day that you work for me, I will give you a dollar as a token of my appreciation."

With the dollar in his pocket, Jason ran home, figuring to himself, Mr. Matroni wants me to come in an extra two days a week now that it's summer. Three dollars a week all summer long, plus the ten from Grandpa, which I will dig up right away — money, money, money!

He ran straight out to the backyard, toward the flowerpot, ready to turn it over and dump out the soil.

But he saw a little something peeking out. It was greenish gray. It was curled up like the first pale leaf of a corn plant. But this wasn't corn.

Jason bent down close, staring. The small greenish-gray tip had the tiniest of scribbly designs on the edge. Very gently he touched it with his finger. It felt tough and strong, like paper. In fact, it felt like the kind of paper that is known as money.

The Counterfeit Scare

"It can't happen," Jason told himself over and over again, hanging onto those words like a mountain climber clutching a rope. *"It can't happen!"*

But the little sprout was as real as the grass beneath his feet. Jason lay down flat on his stomach and stared at the tiny veins in the sprout. Again he touched it, brought his nose close to it. It smelled like all green and growing things.

The ground under him seemed to shift, turning the world at a crazy angle. Once before Jason had felt this way, when he'd ridden too long on the Whirly Bird Ferris Wheel. All the breath had been blown out of his body, leaving him dazed and dizzy, as now. He clutched at the ground, blinked his eyes rapidly, and pinched himself very hard on the arm. At last he sat up, convinced he was not dreaming.

He tried to remember every detail of the night before — the buzzing sound, the full moon, the sea gull. Somehow he had stumbled upon all the right ingredients to make the magic happen. If there had been no rainbow, no dream, or if he had not chanted "In the moonlight hush," today would be an ordinary day. He would be an ordinary person. But he *had* found the secret formula, some ancient wisdom, perhaps, long lost to mankind. The world might have been waiting for a million years for this, for him, Jason Galloway.

Strange, he mused, but maybe not so strange. Deep down he had always had the feeling that he was somehow different from other people.

Oh, how confident, how smug people were when they declared, "Money doesn't grow on trees." Well, the world has been wrong before, thought Jason; hadn't they laughed at Ben Franklin? Didn't they scorn Columbus? He, Jason Galloway, knew the truth about money and trees.

As Jason stood up, wave after wave of excitement sparked through him. Grandpa's talent for making things grow had been passed on to him. The sprout would grow and multiply. With every new harvest he would buy new gifts. A new washer for Mom. A new car for Dad. A decent stroller for Dinah. For himself, a baseball mitt, fishing pole, tackle box. And most important for all of them, he would buy a new house, their dream house.

Never again would he have to wait for the things he wanted. Never again would he have to clip coupons out of magazines for free samples or enter contests for free prizes. From now on, in a way, he'd get everything he wanted absolutely free.

Jason walked around toward the front door, arms lightly outstretched like the wings of a gull. He had never felt so keenly alive. All his senses were sharpened. He could smell the ocean from far below Ocean Park Boulevard. He could hear fog horns groaning from clear across the city near the Golden Gate Bridge. His own hands felt enormous and powerful.

In the record booth at the store Jason sometimes saw a peculiar expression on the faces of teen-agers when they heard a new singing group.

"It's like — wow," they said. "It turns me on."

That was how Jason felt, turned on. As he opened the front door, something told him he'd better concentrate on getting himself turned off.

During dinner Jason remained silent. "I'm going to take a week or two off work to study for the bar exam," Dad said.

Jason hardly heard him. His mind was on more important matters. If the money tree grew as large as an oak, where would he plant it? How long might it take the bills to ripen? If he pinched off some of the

buds, as Grandpa had done with his chrysan-
themums, would the remaining buds grow larger?
Would they bloom into hundred-dollar bills? Even
thousands?

"Ridiculous!" argued his sensible self. "Maybe it's
just a weed, after all." No. No weed on this earth
ever grew with a tiny "10" perfectly engraved on its
tip.

As Jason ate supper, his first shopping list
changed drastically. Why bother with a mitt? Why
not buy the whole team? Jason Galloway, owner of
the San Francisco Giants. As for fishing poles, what
he really needed was one of those boats in Yacht
Harbor. Why not a yacht?

But now a terrible thought brought a dryness to
his throat. How on earth could he explain this sudden wealth to his parents?

"Something wrong, Jason?" Mom asked. "You
look a bit flushed."

Jason felt the sudden urge to tell his parents everything. He glanced at Dad, sober and preoccupied.
Dad even scoffed when Jason sent away for free
samples. "Son, you'll never get something for nothing."

Mom's face was already creased with concern.
She would take him to Dr. Kornblau. He could just
about hear her saying, "Doctor, Jason is having hal-
lucinations. I knew that job would be too much for
him."

The answer seemed simple; just show them the money tree. But despite his confusion, Jason was certain of one thing; he must keep his money tree a secret.

"Speak up, Jason," Dad prodded. "What happened at work today?"

"Mr. Matroni gave me a dollar for working," Jason said, "and he asked me to come in two more days a week now that it's summer vacation."

His parents exchanged a questioning look.

"A dollar a day is hardly anything!" Jason exclaimed. "I mean — is it against the law? That child labor law? Does it mean I can't work for Mr. Matroni anymore?"

He had to keep working, to earn at least a little money to account for all the cash that would grow on the money tree.

"Relax," said Dad. "If the dollar is just — well, not a salary, but a gift, a token..."

"It's a token of appreciation!"

"Well then, that's perfectly all right," said Dad.

Mom frowned. "Three days might be too much, Jason. You need time for play, too."

"No!" Jason cried. "I mean, Mom, it's fun, more fun than playing baseball or anything. Listen, everybody has a certain talent. You've got to do your own thing!" The words came rushing out. "My thing happens to be making money. And a dollar a day adds up fast. You'd be surprised how fast it adds up," he said, his voice rising. "In no time at all you've got ten dollars, then twenty, forty..."

"That's terrific, Jason," Mom said brightly. "We'll count on you in our old age."

"Never mind old age," said Dad with a wink. "How about now?"

Annoyed at Dad's teasing, Jason was terribly tempted to shout out the truth about his money tree. But like an alarm bell, the warning rang in his head: Don't tell! Don't tell!

Mom broke in, seriously now. "You don't know the half of it, Jonathan. The washer broke down again today."

Dad's face suddenly took on the heavy, burdened look Jason didn't like to see. He had seen it often, had heard Dad say grimly, "Well, another setback," as when the car broke down and they had to buy another used one, or when the roof needed fixing. The time Jason fell out of a tree and broke his leg was another setback. Who'd have thought that a broken leg would be so expensive? Before that, Dad got sick and had to go to the hospital for a whole week. In the hospital something else had happened to Dad. As he explained it later, he'd had time to think.

Though Jason was only seven then, Dad had explained it all. "I've made a decision, Jason, and it will affect you. You're a reasonable boy. You should understand. I've decided to go to law school. I've always wanted to be a lawyer. But until now, I never realized how much I wanted it."

"What about the insurance office?" Jason had asked.

"I'll still work there," Dad replied. "I'll go to law school at night. When I'm finished, I'll have a new office and go to court and do all those things I've wanted to do."

Never before had Jason seen that look of longing and excitement on his father's face.

"I think you should go to law school then," Jason had said gravely.

"It might be a bit hard on you," Dad had continued. "We won't have much time together. I'll be in class at night, and on weekends I'll have to study..."

Finally, just a few weeks ago, Dad had graduated. Joyfully, Jason expected immediate release, time with Dad, no more whispering and worry. Then came the shocking announcement. The biggest hurdle still lay ahead.

"Did you think I'd be finished now?" Dad exclaimed. "No. Now I've got to study for the bar exam. Unless I pass that test, I won't be a real lawyer. All these years of study would go down the drain."

Now Dad stood up and stretched. "Back to the books," he said.

"Jonathan," Mom said. "Don't worry about the washer. I've got a few dollars saved, a little nest egg."

"Me, too," Jason said quickly. "And from now on, don't give me fifty cents when I work for Mr. Matroni. I'm tired of hot dogs and cheese sandwiches from the drugstore. I'll take my lunch **along**. And listen, Dad, three dollars a week sure does add up fast."

Dad looked at him for a long moment. It was a strange look, combining astonishment, worry, and tenderness. Then quickly he went back to his studies.

Thick white morning fog rolled in from the ocean. All the backyards way down the street were empty. Shivering, Jason bent down to study his sprout. It had very definitely grown during the night. Now Jason could detect tiny white letters against the green background. "...ITED STATES OF AMER..." The number "10" in the corner was larger, too, and decorated with a fancy swirl.

The small sprout shivered as a gust of wind blew across the yard. Carefully, Jason placed the pot on the narrow strip of concrete between the house and the side fence. Here it would be sheltered. His parents would not see it from the window.

But suppose Mr. Quinley saw it from his yard? Mr. Quinley was a calm, kindly man. But might not the sight of a money tree change him? Money often made people do mean, even violent things. Perhaps Mr. Quinley wouldn't harm him, but word would get around. Crowds of people would come to stare at the money tree. Someone, in a fit of jealousy, might even destroy it.

Jason sat down on the damp lawn, his chin in his

hands. It wasn't going to be easy to raise this money tree. If only somebody could advise him! But the tree had been planted in secret. It must remain a secret. As Jason bent over the sprout once again, it seemed to transmit a clear, strong message. "I am real," it warned, "but only for you. Try to show me off, and I'll dry up and disappear."

Jason whispered to the little sprout, "I'll keep my big mouth shut. And I'll think of a way to hide you."

He would hide the money tree until he had gathered all the cash it was going to produce. Then, somehow he must find a way to give the money to Dad, without getting into trouble. Once Jason had found a dollar on the street, and Dad had given him the third degree. Where money was concerned, even his parents might suspect the worst — that he was a thief.

Maybe that was why Dad objected to getting free things in the mail. Maybe he thought it would lead to wanting more and more things free, until the desire led to stealing.

The morning mail brought Jason three surprises. First he opened a free catalogue of rocket models. Next he received a free picture of a famous hockey star. The third letter was addressed "Homeowner." Mom saved all these for him. As Jason opened it, he suddenly realized that at least one of his problems could be solved.

"TOWN HOUSE COUNTRY HOUSE SWEEPSTAKE,"

the notice proclaimed. "Win your Dream House simply by sending in the enclosed number which has been reserved for you. *You may already have won!* Don't delay. Mail it in today!"

Jason could never resist a printed command. He filled out the coupon and took it to the corner mailbox. That evening he made sure his parents were listening when he told them he'd entered the Town House Country House Sweepstake.

"I hope you win," Dad said absentmindedly. But for the first time, Jason had no intention of winning. He could wait a few weeks or months, then tell his parents that he *had* won. Then there would be no questions about the Dream House he intended to buy with the harvest from his money tree.

That evening, as Jason thumbed through the newspaper, he hummed to himself contentedly. Mom sat beside him on the sofa, working on her Dream House scrapbook. She pasted the picture of a sleek, modern dining set into her book. She caught Jason's eye and held up the book. "Nice?"

"It's O.K., if you like a room all black and white."

"Well, it's a thought. It's good to get lots of ideas."

"Mom, what if we never get that house?"

"Oh — it's fun planning, anyway." She sighed. "It's not the house I want so much. It's really — big trees, better weather, a garden, and a place for you and Dinah to play. The fog here is so depressing."

"Are you depressed? You don't act depressed."

Mom laughed. "Well, that's good."

Now Jason noticed how tired his mother looked, tired from hunting for bargains, from mending and baking to save money. Most nights she was even too tired to work on her scrapbook. She'd have spent the day chasing after other people's kids. That was how she made extra money, her "nest egg."

"It's no trouble having one or two extra little ones," she'd say. But it was trouble. Some afternoons two or three extra babies would be crawling around Mom's feet, pulling out all the pots and pans. They'd eat anything in sight, old shoelaces, even a dead fly in the corner. And Dinah didn't help. Now that she was walking, she roared through the house dumping out wastebaskets, taking things apart. She worked as swiftly and quietly as a safecracker. Her crimes were detected by the wreckage she left behind. Her specialty was throwing things down the toilet.

"Things will get better soon," Jason said cautiously.

"Sure. You don't have to worry about money, Jason. We've got all we really need. Anything else would be just frills."

Jason finished the funnies, then turned the page. A picture of three grim-looking men caught his eye. The headline said, "Counterfeiters Caught!"

Quickly he scanned the article, and his heart gave a frightened lurch. Unwittingly, Jason gasped.

"What's wrong?" Mom asked.

"Uh — the police caught some counterfeiters. They were printing fake money in their basement."

Mom nodded. "Yes, I read that."

"What will happen to them?"

"They'll go to prison."

"How long?"

"Ten years, maybe fifteen."

"But they didn't hurt anybody!" Jason cried.

"Of course they did. Counterfeiting is like stealing. They were trying to buy things with money that has no real value. People can't just go around making their own money! What a mess we'd be in! Anyhow, it's against the law."

Jason felt hot, then cold, then plain scared. "Planting a money tree," he told himself firmly, "is not anything like printing phony money in a basement. It's not anything like counterfeiting."

But a calm, reasonable voice from somewhere inside him seemed to retort, "Oh, isn't it?"

The First Harvest

The money tree was limp. The poor sprout hung over to one side, as if it were dying. Jason poked the hard, dry soil. His plant needed moisture, but how much? All the gardening books in the world couldn't tell him how to raise a money tree.

"Look it up in the encyclopedia!" Dad often exclaimed in answer to Jason's questions. Once Grandpa, hearing this reply, had said mildly, "Some of the most important answers are not found in books, Jonathan. Sometimes you just have to do what *feels* right."

Now Jason turned on the hose to just a trickle and let the water seep slowly into the pot. The water bubbled up with a small murmuring sound, like a sigh. At once the sprout seemed to straighten; the edge of the leaf felt crisp and firm again.

Jason went to Mr. Matroni's, and by the time he returned home, his sprout was nearly an inch long. But even more wonderful, the stem was beginning to divide, and two new buds were forming. If the stem kept dividing, if new buds kept appearing, if they grew even faster as he picked the ripe bills...

The first bud was beginning to unfurl. On it were inscribed the words "legal tender." *Tender*, Jason mused. Was this something new, something found only on homegrown bills, like labels on packages, "Fragile," "Handle with Care"?

Back in his room, Jason thumbed through the dictionary. *Tender*. Soft or delicate, it said. Hastily he reached for the one-dollar bill he had earned from Mr. Matroni. It, too, was imprinted, "This note is legal tender..."

Puzzled, he read on. *Something tendered or offered, especially money, as in payment.*

Legal money! Legal payment! He rushed to the kitchen, scooped up Dinah, and whirled her around in his arms. "Ho! Ho! Ho!" he boomed in his deepest voice, making her laugh and squeal.

"What's that racket?" came a roar from the den. "Sounds like a Santa Claus convention."

With a whack the afternoon paper struck the front door, hurled there by the paper boy speeding along on his bike. Jason brought in the paper and was

about to turn to the comics when the large picture of a twenty-dollar bill caught his eye. The caption read, "Could you have spotted this counterfeit bill?"

On the bill in the picture were the very same words, "This note is legal tender for all debts public and private."

Jason felt sick. He stumbled into the counter, banging his funny bone. It ached and tingled and sent shooting pains through his whole arm.

Wildly he rummaged through the refrigerator, dug out five oranges, and frantically began to squeeze them.

His mother smiled knowingly.

When the glass was brimming full, Jason knocked loudly at Dad's door. "Come on out," he called. "Take a break. I made you fresh orange juice."

It worked like a charm. Dad could never resist fresh orange juice.

"Dad, I need advice," Jason began, "about the law."

"The law," his father murmured wearily, "is a seamless web."

"Dad, please! Every time I ask you something about the law you start talking about seamless webs."

"A seamless web," Dad continued, "complicated, every part connected to another..."

"Dad, if a thing isn't against the law, is it all right to do it?"

Dad's eyes snapped open. "What do you mean? Be specific. Give me the facts."

"Can I keep a cow in our yard if there's no law against it?" Jason asked.

"There *is* a law against it. Our deed says that..."

"Can I keep a dog in our yard if there is no law against it?" Jason persisted.

"Yes. You can keep anything if there is no law against it." Dad's eyes narrowed suspiciously. "What are you keeping out in the backyard?"

"Nothing! I'm just giving you an example."

"You've been spending an awful lot of time out there, Jason. Is it some kind of pet?"

Alerted by the word "pet," Mom asked anxiously, "Jason, have you brought home a stray cat?"

"Or a dog?" Dad added. "A cow?"

"No! It's..." Jason sighed. "It's just a snail. A snail in a jar."

"A snail!" they both exclaimed. Mom rushed to feel Jason's forehead. "Are you serious? Are you sick?"

"What kind of pet is that?" Dad demanded.

"A quiet one!" Jason snapped. It was just a small, stupid lie, and they'd forced him into it, after all.

"You never answer my questions," Jason grumbled.

"Very well." Dad drew himself up straight and said in a ringing tone, "In general, if a thing is not forbidden by law, then it's allowed. The law," he said loudly, "is built on cases that actually happened. When lawyers take a case to court they find out what was done in a similar case. That is called *precedent*."

"But what if it's the first time anything like it ever happened?" Jason asked.

"Nothing is completely new or different," Dad replied.

"It could be!"

"Then the court does what is fair," said Dad, and he promptly went back to his studies.

"Oh, the law is a seamless web!" Jason moaned to himself, feeling hopelessly caught in the tangled threads. He imagined himself on trial, exclaiming, "But, Your Honor, it *said* 'legal tender' right on the bill."

Sternly, the judge confronts him. "My boy, just because a phrase is printed, does that make it true? I can take a box of matches and label it *candy*. Does that make it so?"

There was only one way to find out whether or not his money-tree bill was genuine. As soon as it was ripe, he'd have to spend it. The threads of that web called the law seemed to tighten around Jason's throat. If the bill wasn't genuine, it would be a crime to spend it. But how could it be a crime if there was no law against it? Precedent! Jason heard echo upon echo of the word. What was the precedent for a money tree? Only one thing came close. Counterfeiting.

It was time. The bill had bloomed now. It hung curled like an ice-cream cone, fastened to the branch by its point. On the green side were the words, "In God We Trust."

"Jason! Jason!" Mom's face at the window made him jump. "We're going out for a ride," she called. "Come on."

Inside Dinah was already bundled up. "Get your jacket, Jason," Mom told him. "Dad's taking a couple of hours off. We'll drive up to Marin County and get some sunshine."

"I — I'm not going," Jason said, bending down over the Sunday funnies.

"Not going? You always want to go out, and Dad..."

"I told Dave I'd play baseball with him."

"But, Jason..."

"Leave him alone, Liz," Dad spoke up. "He's old enough to stay here without us."

"But, Jonathan..."

Jason heard them murmuring, "...big boy ...needs privacy...of course I'd rather have him... we have so little time together."

The rest was drowned out by Dinah's happy squeals. "Go bye-bye!"

Why, Jason raged to himself, why was there always such turmoil before anyone left this house? "Go!" he wanted to shout, to push them out the door. "I want to be alone!"

Mom ran back for Dinah's blanket. Dad forgot his glasses, then his keys. Then Mom remembered she ought to pull a chunk of frozen hamburger out of the freezer.

"Good-bye," Jason said at last, walking with them to the door. Then, with a sinking feeling, he heard a gay whistle, and Mom called cheerfully, "Here comes Dave with his baseball bat. Have fun, Jason."

He was stuck. He would have sent Dave away, but it took Dad forever to get the old car started, and Mom was watching from the car window.

"I'll go get my mitt," Jason mumbled, trying to stall.

"I brought an extra one," Dave said. "Come on! We'll get some of the little kids and play 500. You're first up this time, remember?"

First up was too good to turn down, and the car was still sputtering at the curb. At last his parents took off, but by then the game was in full swing. Those clumsy little kids dropped every fly, and time was wasting away while Jason, gritting his teeth, finished his ups. Then, of course, he couldn't just walk away. Oh, no. "Bad sport," they'd yell after him. "Take your ups and run!"

Jason dragged himself through the game for nearly an hour. At last, fog turned to drizzle, and from the outfield Jason gave a great sneeze.

"I'm catching cold!" he cried. "I've got to go inside."

Inside he ran, then out the back door. And as he ran, all his doubts multiplied. Was he, in this moment, headed toward a lifetime of crime? Would he recall someday from his prison cell, "It all started that Sunday in Silverview, when I tried to get something for nothing."

He ran toward the flowerpot. Should he cut the bill with a clipper and risk cutting out a piece? Should he pull it off and risk yanking out the whole sprout?

As Jason approached his money tree, all worries left him. He should have known. Nature is orderly. No need for guess work. Lying loosely on top of the soil in the flowerpot was his first ten-dollar bill, neatly severed from its stem.

Reverently Jason held it in his hand, then flattened it against his knee. It was still slightly damp. The edges kept curling up as Dinah's little fists had always curled up when she was a newborn baby.

But this was not a baby bill. As far as he could tell, it was a full-fledged, genuine adult ten-dollar bill, and perfect in every way.

The Teller and the Tax Man

Jason set out for work on Monday morning with the ten-dollar bill in his pocket and fear in his heart. "Be prepared for a huge disappointment," he told himself. "A genuine money tree is too good to be true."

After a long, painful struggle, Jason had reached a decision. If his newly grown ten-dollar bill turned out to be a fake, he would have to destroy the money tree. For better or worse, he would soon find out. This morning he would take time off from Matroni's to go to the Silverview Bank. Who would know better than a banker whether money was counterfeit or real?

By the time Jason got to the bank, it was near noon, the rush hour. The line was long; the bank was hot and stuffy. His back itched; he got a stomach-ache. From above, like a tremendous eye, a large round reflector beamed down at him. A sign gave warning, "This place of business is guarded by ELECTRO-EYE." It gave Jason the creeps. Was it against the law just to be *carrying* a phony bill?

Near the door stood the bank guard, chatting with customers, pretending not to notice the money being passed back and forth across the counters. It was just an act. That guard didn't miss a thing. In a flash his bulging pistol could be drawn, leveled coldly at someone's heart.

Four people to go. Three. Two. Jason thrust his hands into his pockets, wiping away the sweat on his palms. He stared at the sign "Teller." A strange title — what did it mean? Suddenly Jason knew. They tell. They tell everything, every slight suspicion.

Now, with only one person ahead of him, Jason felt hot all over. If only he could stop sweating! He had seen an old TV movie where the crook got caught simply because the detective's dog picked him out from a whole group of innocent men. And how? Sweat.

"May I help you?"

Jason cleared his throat. The momentary pause brought an inspiration. "Miss — er — Teller," he began, "would you mind showing me one of your ten-dollar bills? That is — um — I want to see a 1934 ten-dollar bill. If you don't mind. I'll give it right back. In a few minutes." Jason managed a crooked smile, while the teller continued to stare at him as if his whole head were transparent and she could see wheels spinning there.

"No," the teller retorted. "You cannot borrow a ten-dollar bill. This bank does not make loans to people under twenty-one years of age. Next!"

"Please!" Jason persisted. He reached into his pocket and took out the money-tree bill. "What I really want to know is — is about this bill."

The man behind Jason lit a cigar. Clouds of evil-smelling smoke settled around Jason's head.

The teller picked up Jason's bill, dangling it from her fingers as if it were a live spider.

"You see," said Jason, "my grandfather gave it to me. And what I want to know is, is it all right?"

The teller looked shocked. "You think your grandfather gave you a *bad* ten-dollar bill?"

"No. It's just that it's so old."

The teller glanced over her shoulder. "Did your grandfather say anything to make you believe it might not be a true bill?"

"Oh, no," exclaimed Jason. "He couldn't have. My grandfather's dead. He left it to me."

If even a small speck of kindness existed in the teller's nature, it was all gone now. Angrily she looked at the bill. Her movements, her voice, suggested complete disgust at any boy who would accuse his dead grandfather of having left him a phony bill.

"It's fine," she said stiffly. "Just fine. Next!"

"Fine! Just fine!" All afternoon while Jason

played records for the teen-agers and showed models to the little kids, those words sang through his head. "Fine. Just fine!"

If that sharp-eyed teller could find nothing wrong with the money-tree bill, then it was perfectly legal. Legal tender. Even Dad wouldn't be able to argue with that.

All afternoon Jason's thoughts drifted from daydream to daydream. Money. He envisioned money in stacks, piles, boxes, bags, bundles. He would gather it all, hide it well, until the tree's growing season was over. And Jason would not be greedy. He would not allow the tree to fade, like a camellia bush, and then bloom again the following spring. Just one good season was all he asked.

While he dusted the shelves, Jason did a little figuring in his head. His goal was a cool million. If he began with ten and doubled that amount every day, how long would it take for him to become a millionaire?

"Mr. Matroni," Jason asked, "may I use the adding machine in the back room?"

"Sure."

Three times Jason repeated his calculations. The result was even more fantastic than he had imagined.

This morning he had seen two new buds nearly ready to bloom, and the two stems dividing themselves again. If the buds continued to bloom daily, like squash, if the stems continued to divide, in just seventeen days Jason would have exactly one million, three hundred and ten thousand, seven hundred and ten dollars.

It was staggering. How would he gather it? Where keep it? How spend it? Staggering!

Jason staggered toward the door.

"Hey, Jason!" Mr. Matroni called him back. "Be sure to come in on Thursday, eh?"

Thursday...eighty dollars by Thursday..."Uh — sure, Mr. Matroni," Jason mumbled.

"Good. I'll really need you. I'll be busy most of the day with the IRS man."

"The IRS man?"

"Internal Revenue Service," said Mr. Matroni proudly. "The tax man. You know, they come out and check on people's taxes once in a while. The President of the United States in Washington, D.C., has to make sure nobody's hiding anything."

"Hiding?" Jason echoed dully.

"Taxes," Mr. Matroni repeated. "You know. You make money, and the President of the United States has to get his share to run the country with. Understand?"

Jason rubbed his eyes. "How — how much is the tax?"

"That depends on how much you make. The more you make, the more taxes you pay. If you make $60,000, you have to pay nearly half of it in taxes."

A tight feeling began to close in on Jason's throat. "What if somebody makes a million?" he whispered.

Mr. Matroni laughed. "Jason, don't worry. One dollar from me for working a whole day won't make you a millionaire, not in a lifetime." He reached into the cash register and presented Jason with a dollar.

"But what if a person did make a million?" Jason persisted. "I guess a whole lot of it would go for taxes."

"You bet. It's those millionaires that the Internal Revenue Service men really go after. You read about that sometimes, rich people trying to hide money from Internal Revenue. But they always catch 'em."

"What happens to them?" Jason breathed.

"Jail. Listen, are you worried about something? Don't worry. I always report all the money I earn. I am a one hundred percent honest and good American. Let the tax man come! He'll find out. I'm clean." And Mr. Matroni smiled a bright, clean smile and said, "See you Thursday, partner."

Outside, a rare burst of sunlight beamed down at Jason, blindingly bright. Tax man! Flashing badge, gravel voice. "Aha! What have we here!" Tax man, sweltering courtroom, lawyer jumps up to plead, "Your Honor, he's just a child. He didn't know better." The D.A. shouts back, "Ignorance is no excuse!" Bang goes the gavel. The judge opens one eye and pronounces, "Guilty!"

As if a hundred hounds were breathing down his back, Jason began to run. The tax man was coming Thursday to Matroni's; Friday, where? Did he make his way down the street, like the Fuller Brush man?

Jason ran full steam, crossed the street, and fell flat on his face. Someone's rusted, forgotten skate had snagged him, just the way the tax man would trip him up soon.

Quick tears sprang to Jason's eyes, half from the pain of his skinned knee, half from fear and misery.

"Jason!" his mother exclaimed when she saw him. "What's wrong?"

"Nothing!"

"Who's chasing you?"

"Nobody."

"But, Jason, you're crying and shaking...why?"

"The tax man is coming to Matroni's!" he cried. "Some nut left a skate on the sidewalk; I could have gotten *killed*. If there's a knock at the door," he panted, "don't answer it! It might not be the Fuller Brush man."

Later, soothed and bandaged, Jason heard his parents talking in worried tones. "He's completely exhausted. Maybe this job is too much for him."

"He does seem nervous and jumpy..."

"He's always been such a sensible boy...reliable...a good boy."

In the darkness of his room Jason trembled. "That's what they all say," he thought. Once on the TV news he had seen a young man convicted for murder. His parents huddled beside him, weeping. They said, "He was always such a good boy!"

A One Hundred Percent
Honest Man

Making certain that his parents were asleep, Jason crept out into the backyard. The white beam from his flashlight drifted back at him like a snowy mist. Not a single star shone through the billowing fog.

He directed his light onto the flowerpot, expecting to see two beautiful bills. Instead he saw only a naked branch, ghostly white and shivering.

A cat yeowled from behind the fence, and Jason jumped, smothering a cry. "Robber! Where's my money? Stupid!" he said to himself. "What would a cat want with ten-dollar bills? Cats don't eat greens."

Now, curved across the cement, Jason saw a silvery path, a snail trail. Only inches away from his foot the snail rested, fat and juicy. One antenna reached forward, searching for something crisp and green to eat.

In this eerie white world of fog it seemed entirely possible, even logical. Ripe ten-dollar bills, lettuce-crisp and green, had provided supper for the snail. Angrily, Jason picked up the snail and turned it over, looking for telltale green sticky stuff. The antennae wavered protestingly, not guilty! In that moment Jason saw his two precious ten-dollar bills. They lay pressed flat against the fence, held there by the wind. Jason stared, dropped the snail, pulled off his bills, and stuffed them into his pocket.

Clammy cold droplets covered his face. He sighed deeply with relief. He must never let that happen again. Suppose his bills had blown into the Quinleys' yard? How could he possibly explain to Mr. Quinley why he was snooping around in the night like a cat burglar? "Oh, pardon me, Mr. Quinley. I believe my money tree is blowing bills over into your yard." He could just see himself trying to get away with that.

Clearly, he needed a proper routine. He must be sure to gather the bills as soon as they fell. He must find time to water his plant every day. Soon he would have to transplant it into a larger pot. And, above all, he must hide it, somehow, from the prying eyes of his neighbors.

No sooner had Jason watered his money tree than he noticed an improvement. The stem, now the thickness of a pencil, seemed to swell and straighten. Everything was proceeding according to plan. The original stem had divided itself into two branches. These had, in turn, divided. Each of the four branches bore a tight, small green bud. Jason was not surprised. But he was filled with gratitude and whispered, "Thank you!"

Back in his room, Jason spread all his money out on his bed. Three dollars from Mr. Matroni, and thirty dollars from the money tree. Thirty-three dollars! Never in his entire life had he possessed such a fortune.

The following day Jason saw that his next harvest would be delayed. Well, that made sense. Four buds drawing strength from a single stem would take longer to ripen.

"Tomorrow," Jason told himself. And when tomorrow came, he actually watched the bills as they slowly bloomed. Just before suppertime he saw them burst wide open and fall.

"Hey, Jason!" came a shout over the fence, and Dave Parker's eyes stared at him, round with excitement. "Guess what?"

Quickly Jason put the bills in his pocket and ran to the fence.

"Whatcha got?" Dave asked.

"Nothing."

"I see you," Dave said accusingly, "bending down all the time. Last night and the night before," he said, "I looked out of my window and saw you with a flashlight."

"So? Don't I have a right to go out in my own yard?"

"I read about a man who shot his own son," Dave declared. "He heard someone prowling around, thought it was a burglar. Shot him dead."

"Is that all you wanted to tell me?" Jason scoffed.

"No. Guess what?"

Jason clenched his fists, exasperated by Dave's continual "guess what." Strange, he had never noticed it before. Now it irritated him, and he wondered how it had happened that they became best friends.

"Tell me," Jason said. "I don't have time to play guessing games."

"My dad said I could invite you to go to Clear Lake with us this weekend!" Dave exclaimed.

Jason stood motionless, silent.

"We'll go boating, fishing, hiking."

"Thanks. But, no thanks."

"Are you kidding? Don't you want to go?"

"I can't. See, I have to go to work on Saturday."

"Won't Mr. Matroni let you off for once?"

"It's not just that," Jason said, eyes downcast. "I've got to stay home. I've got things to do."

"Oh, Clear Lake," thought Jason longingly. "Sparkling blue water, tall pines, evening campfire under the stars!" But he had responsibilities. If he went away, who would tend his money tree? "A

wealthy man," thought Jason with a sigh, "is never completely free."

"Oh, I see," said Dave stiffly.

"Thanks anyway," said Jason sadly. He'd never be able to make Dave understand. If he tried to explain, invent another excuse, he'd only get tripped up.

At dinner his mother, trying to appear casual, remarked, "Mrs. Parker told me Dave invited you to Clear Lake this weekend and you refused."

Jason squirmed. His discomfort quickly turned to anger. "I don't want to go to Clear Lake with Dave Parker!" he snapped.

"I thought you two were good friends," said Mom.

Dad spoke up. "I think Jason's showing a good sense of responsibility. He doesn't want to disappoint Mr. Matroni. Isn't that right, son?"

Jason nodded. He felt very virtuous. And that night, alone in his room, the sight of seventy-three dollars spread out before him almost made him forget the delights of Clear Lake. He was rich! He threw the bills up in the air and watched them flutter down like leaves. Money! Power! Pleasure! Just wait. There would be plenty of money left over after he bought a house, a car, and everything else he wanted, for a little cabin in the woods at Clear Lake.

Awed, Jason stared at himself in the mirror. He alone had found what everyone is always searching for. The miner with his pick yearns for that one big strike. The gardener, sinking his spade into the earth, secretly dreams of hitting a gushing oil well. Children skipping down the street peer into gutters, looking for coins from heaven with which they will fill their pockets. And here, in cold, dingy Silverview, stood the one person who had finally hit the jackpot.

"I," said Jason aloud, "am the happiest, luckiest boy in the world."

But tomorrow the tax man was coming to Matroni's. From there he'd make his way down the street to Jason's house. They were a clever crew, those tax men. They had ways of finding hidden money. And the tax on money-tree money was probably sky-high.

He scooped up his bills. "Spend it!" shrieked the inner voice, a poltergeist, perhaps. Yes, he would begin to spend it first thing tomorrow morning. He would buy that Super-Duper fishing pole at Matroni's for $38.95. His parents wouldn't know how much it had cost. He would let them think it was cheaper and that Mr. Matroni had given him a discount as another "token of appreciation."

Mr. Matroni would offer him a ten percent discount because he worked there. "No thanks, Mr. Matroni," he would say grandly. "I'll pay the full price. Business is business."

"Business is business," said Mr. Matroni, with his arm around Jason's shoulder. "Every businessman should have a reliable partner. I'd like you to meet my partner, Mr. Zuckernick." To Jason he said, "Mr. Zuckernick is the tax man I told you about. Internal Revenue Service. Sent by the President of the United States in Washington, D.C."

"Put 'er there," said Mr. Zuckernick, extending his hand.

"My partner," continued Mr. Matroni. "Jason..."

"Just call me Jason!" interrupted Jason. There was no sense in telling this IRS man his last name. He'd get to the Galloways soon enough.

Mr. Zuckernick was totally bald, round faced, and much younger than Jason had expected. And Jason soon discovered that Mr. Zuckernick had a peculiar habit of ending nearly every sentence with a strange little laugh that wasn't really a laugh at all.

"Glad to meet you, Jason, ha-ha. So you're Mr. Matroni's partner. Did you invest in the business? Ha-ha."

"No, sir," said Jason. He almost added a "ha-ha" of his own, but caught himself in time. One must not seem disrespectful to an employee of the President of the United States.

"Does Jason earn a salary?" asked Mr. Zuckernick.

"No, not really," replied Mr. Matroni. "I haven't deducted Jason's pay on my income tax. What he earns is — well, just a token of my appreciation. He's certainly worth more than a dollar a day."

"I see. A friendly arrangement, ha-ha. How long

54

have you been working here, Jason?"

"Nearly two months," Jason replied, "but I just started getting paid last week."

Instantly, Jason recognized his mistake. With forty-one dollars in his pocket, he had intended to buy the Super-Duper fishing pole today. It didn't take an IRS genius to figure out that a kid like him didn't normally go around with over forty bucks in his pocket. Savings? Allowance? No — his torn jeans were proof enough that his parents couldn't afford that kind of money. The fishing pole would have to wait.

Jason felt like the child in the nursery rhyme who was told he could go swimming "but don't go near the water." Maybe, like those folks in Ohio, he, too, was being haunted by a poltergeist. Wouldn't it be just like a poltergeist to give him a money tree and then not let him spend any money?

Jason gazed longingly at the fishing pole while he caressed the bills in his pocket. It was getting unbearably warm in the store. Soon he'd have to remove his jacket. What to do with the money? The pockets of his jeans were worn through. The pocket of his jacket was too shallow; the bills might accidentally fall out.

In the back room Jason hung up his jacket and put on the smock. The smock had pockets, but they never stayed flat. They billowed out so that anything in them was clearly visible.

"Jason!" called Mr. Matroni. "Please come out here and help these boys."

Quickly, Jason took off his shoe and slipped his wad of bills inside. It felt odd to be walking on forty-one dollars, but at least his money was right under foot.

Tending the store all alone, Jason was in his glory. While Mr. Matroni was busy with the tax man, Jason was in charge. With a pencil tucked behind his ear, he took long, efficient strides across the store, and he could almost hear the voice of the commentator making a documentary film. "The shop clerk seems to be everywhere at once, a model of tact and alertness. He sells, wraps, checks the merchandise...this clerk of eleven, going on twelve, does not forget to smile. He knows that a cheerful clerk makes a happy customer and that happy customers come back."

Zing went the cash drawer. Snap, he opened the bag. "Thank you!" and a smiling "Come again."

Then in walked Dave Parker to buy some fish hooks. "Guess what?" he began. "My dad's gonna let me try his casting rod."

Jason wanted to retort, "Guess what? I've got a money tree growing in my yard." Instead he smiled his shop-clerk smile and ducked down for the fish hooks.

In his mind's eye Jason envisioned a fat round bobber, felt the tug of a big one, and saw the streak of silvery fins as he pulled the fish in a wide arc from the water.

"Want to go fishing at Lake Serra some day?" he asked.

"O.K.," Dave replied coolly.

They had fished at Lake Serra before, sitting on a patch of dirt at the side of the road that wound around the small lake. It wasn't bad, if you ignored the cars. Sometimes, if they could sit under a tree, it was almost like being in the country. The only trouble was that they never caught any fish. Once in a while they pulled up a slimy old sock or a tin can.

"I'll bring you home a fish," Dave promised, smiling generously, and Jason could tell he had been instructed, "Now, you be nice to that poor Jason Galloway."

"It's kind of nice," Dave added, "to catch a fish when you go fishing."

"I guess it would be," Jason mused. "Maybe next time," he added, "I could go with you to Clear Lake."

"Sure. Well — gotta go."

By lunchtime Jason's foot was throbbing. He decided to go home and put his money away. But Mr. Matroni had something else in mind.

"We'll all eat together," he said, nodding toward the lunch bag Mr. Zuckernick had brought. "Jason, you run out and get a six pack of soda pop. The treat's on me," he added grandly.

"My dear Mr. Matroni!" Mr. Zuckernick drew

back stiffly, as if he'd been outrageously insulted. "I cannot possibly accept. Employees of the federal government," he said sternly, "are not allowed to accept favors. We are not allowed to engage in any activity which might..."

"I understand perfectly!" broke in Mr. Matroni. "Forgive me, Mr. Zuckernick. Jason, this is a one hundred percent honest man."

When Jason returned with the soda pop, Mr. Matroni called out, "Jason, is something wrong with your leg? You're limping."

Jason froze. Mr. Zuckernick, too, was staring at him.

"I guess it's that old injury again," Jason said.

"Old injury? Ha-ha."

"I broke my leg once," Jason said rapidly. That was true. But he felt a stab of conscience at confronting a "one hundred percent honest man" with such a lie. The leg he had broken never bothered him at all. And the money was, in fact, in the shoe on the opposite foot.

"Sit down, Jason," said Mr. Matroni. He took Mr. Zuckernick's quarter, then handed him a bottle of soda pop. "Now, Jason, this is your chance. Mr. Zuckernick is a one hundred percent qualified Internal Revenue Service tax man. If you have any questions about taxes or money, he's the man who can answer them."

Mr. Zuckernick's smiling round face took on a pinkish glow.

Mr. Matroni leaned foreward, waiting.

Mr. Zuckernick leaned back, glowing.

Jason's foot ached; his thoughts were muddled. The overhead light stung his eyes; the heat was on! Honesty! The word exploded in his brain. Perhaps honesty was the best policy, after all, and here was his chance to question an expert.

"Ask me," urged Mr. Zuckernick.

"Ask him," persisted Mr. Matroni.

Jason licked his lips. He'd confess, bring matters to a head. Maybe Dad didn't know everything about the law and taxes. Maybe the government had made a special rule for money that was suddenly found in extraordinary ways. Maybe there was no tax at all on money gotten by pure luck.

Jason asked, "Mr. Zuckernick, suppose a person gets a lot of money unexpectedly. That is — have you ever heard of — a money tree?"

Mr. Zuckernick didn't hesitate for a moment. "Sure."

"You have?"

"As a matter of fact, my parents gave me one last Christmas."

"They did?"

"My wife and I used it all to pay for our vacation."

"You mean you used it all up?"

"Well, yes. We needed the cash for our trip. Maybe we should have waited for it to grow more, ha-ha."

"Did you — did you have to pay a tax on it?"

"Oh, no. It was a gift. Gifts are tax free, ha-ha, if they're under $3,000."

"My grandfather left me a ten-dollar bill," Jason said hastily. He was trembling and sweating, but Mr. Zuckernick didn't seem to notice.

"Don't worry about that. It's yours, free and clear, ha-ha."

"Ha-ha," Jason echoed, almost laughing aloud with relief.

Mr. Zuckernick carefully wiped his lips with a paper napkin. "Any more questions?"

"One more," said Jason. "Where did your parents get the money tree?"

"They bought it at a gift shop in the city. Cromwell's, I think."

Problems in the Pumpkin Patch

It had been a terrific shock, and all afternoon Jason had gone about his duties like a sleepwalker. At last it all fell into place. It was just one of those things that some people know but won't talk about unless they're asked. Like witchcraft, he thought, or ESP. Most people don't believe in it. But if you just happened to ask the right person, a real witch, for example, they'd tell you the truth. But who'd have thought that bald, round-face-glowing Mr. Zuckernick was one of *them*?

As Jason sat at the edge of the bathtub soaking his foot, he wondered how many others in the world shared his secret. All over the earth a chosen few people did have money trees. They grew secretly in greenhouses, in orchards, in vegetable gardens. Why had he never seen one? Because they were camouflaged, of course. If you want to hide a tree, plant it among lots of other growing things. That was exactly what he himself would have done if his yard wasn't so bare.

As for a money tree being sold at Cromwell's, that, too, was obvious. The "better stores" often sold unusual items. They were kept in the back room or under the counter, away from the common customer. But if you knew what to ask for, the clerk would bring it to you, smiling and bowing with respect.

Jason had shopped at Cromwell's once before, with his Great-Aunt Tilda. She was so wealthy that she never carried any money at all; she just flashed gold and white credit cards in front of the clerks' eyes.

That day at Cromwell's, Aunt Tilda had taken the saleslady aside and whispered, "I've come for that imported Hungarian china, my dear. *You* remember."

"Yes, yes, of course," the saleslady's skirts rustled as she darted off to reappear with a large box mysteriously labeled, "XB-30578H."

Naturally, one had to be rich to *buy* a money tree. With extraordinary luck and talent, a few people, like him, were able to grow their own, from scratch.

Jason dried his foot and lay down on his bed, pretending to be asleep. He waited for a full half hour after his mother had come in to check his window. Then he crept out into the backyard.

Only one ten-dollar bill lay on the soil for him to take. The other seven still hung from their stems. Jason scanned them with the aid of his flashlight. He stared, dismayed. One of them was deformed. It was developing a two-headed Alexander Hamilton.

Reluctantly, Jason picked it off and threw it into the garbage can. Well, even nature makes mistakes, he thought. He had heard about a two-headed lizard, a three-legged duck. Still, he was worried. He needed the advice of an expert money-tree grower. Who would be better qualified than the merchant who sold money trees? He must get to Cromwell's in the city.

Jason was joyful, though not entirely surprised, when the very next morning Dad said, "I have to go to the city today to look up something in the law library. Want to come with me?"

"Sure. Could we stop at Cromwell's?"

"I suppose so. What do you want at Cromwell's?"

"I heard it's a good gift store. I thought I'd look for a present for Mom."

"A whole month ahead of time? Well, I guess it doesn't hurt to start early. That's the sensible way.

Now, you just do something quiet. I'll be ready in a few minutes."

Jason made his bed and then went to stand by Dad's door.

"Five more minutes!" Dad called out.

Jason polished his shoes, rode Dinah piggyback, then waited at Dad's door.

"Just another five minutes!"

"If you're not ready," Jason said, "I'll go over to Mr. Matroni's for a little while." He would buy the Super-Duper fishing pole today.

"Don't go! I'll be ready in five minutes."

Jason sighed. "O.K. I'll be outside — with my snail."

Outside, Jason watered his tree, bent down, and whispered softly, "Dear money tree, keep on growing." He had read somewhere that even plants respond to kindness. Sweet words and soft music made them grow better. Very softly Jason hummed "America the Beautiful." It seemed a fitting choice, in view of six pictures of the Treasury Building and *E Pluribus Unum*.

From the window Dad's voice roared out, "Jason! Aren't you ready yet? Why aren't you ever ready to leave?"

At last they were under way. They drove through Silverview, up the hill to Ocean Park Boulevard. From here the houses looked like large dominoes stacked side by side. One push and they'd all come tumbling down like a heap of little boxes.

They drove onto the freeway, past the sooty, puffing factories, toward the broad avenues and pillared buildings of Civic Center. For a long time they drove without speaking. Jason glanced at Dad; he was smiling to himself.

"What are you thinking, Dad?"

I'm nearly through. It's been a long haul, Jason. Just between you and me," Dad said, "there were times I didn't think I'd make it. But now there's only the bar exam, and then..."

"I guess you'll be glad to have some free time," Jason remarked.

"You know it!"

"Wouldn't it be great," Jason began, "if we had loads of money and you never had to work?"

"Great! I'd just lie around in the sun all day, maybe take up surfing. You and I would walk along Ocean Beach for hours and hours. Of course, you wouldn't work at Mr. Matroni's anymore."

"I like working for Mr. Matroni!" Jason objected. "I'd still want to do that. But if we had some extra money, a big nest egg..."

"A nest egg is nice to have," Dad agreed. Abruptly, he shifted his attention to the rush of traffic and the whistling, waving policeman in the middle of the street.

"When you pass the bar exam," Jason said, "I'm going to give you a present. You'll be surprised."

But Dad had stopped listening, and Jason envisioned the scene a few weeks from now. He
would walk slowly toward Dad, struggling with the
huge laundry basket, filled to the brim with ten-
dollar bills.

"Jason!" Dad shouts in alarm. "Where did you
get all that money?"

"Well, you might not believe this..."

"Try me!"

"It's from my money tree."

Dad scratches his head and murmurs, "I've
heard about such things, superstitions, I thought. I
never dreamed that anyone actually..."

"Not many people know about it, Dad."

"But, son, is it legal?"

"Yup. Legal tender — it says so right here."

"What about taxes, son?"

"No taxes. I got that straight from the IRS. It
all started with Grandpa's ten-dollar bill. Gifts
aren't taxable. The gift just grew, that's all. Of
course, it took faith and talent and hard work."

"My son, you are faithful and talented and hard-
working."

"Actually, Dad, this is from a 'do-it-yourself'
money tree. I could have bought one at Cromwell's,
but I thought you'd like it better if I grew my
own."

"I do, son. Oh, I do."

Abruptly, Jason came out of his reverie as they
pulled up at the law library. When Dad was fin-

ished, they went out for a milkshake, then to Cromwell's. It was an experience Jason would never forget.

Afterward, on the way home again, Jason closed his eyes tightly, pretending to be asleep. Never before had he felt so foolish, so humiliated.

Dad had come into the store with him. Boldly, Jason had stepped up to the display case, pretending that he was just browsing.

At last a thin, long-legged clerk in a black suit walked up to them. Dad, nodding toward Jason, said, "I think this boy might want some help."

Jason drew the clerk aside and whispered. "I've heard that you sell" — he glanced about, and the clerk bent down to catch the words — "money trees."

"Yes, sir!" The clerk glanced at Dad, who was half turned away, looking at some watches. Bobbing from the waist, the clerk whispered, "I understand," and motioned Jason to come behind the counter.

The clerk kneeled, folded his legs under himself, and reached deep inside the shelf. "I think I've got just what you're looking for. Ah, yes — here it is."

Jason blinked several times. In his hand the clerk held a ten-inch tall, flat plastic tree mounted into a square of polished wood.

"Is this the kind of money tree you had in mind, son?"

"Not exactly," Jason mumbled, feeling his face turn beet-red.

"You see," the clerk continued, "you slip the bills into these little slots at the tips of the branches. The bills look like leaves. It makes an attractive gift, and a practical one, too." And then, to Jason's horror, the clerk gave a little laugh. "Ha-ha."

"Are you getting car sick? You look a little queasy," Dad said as they drove home. "Just open your window and lie back."

The shock of seeing that plastic money tree left Jason feeling as if someone had shaken him, hard. He let himself drift with the steady purring of the motor, the gentle motion of the car. Then suddenly he was struck with the enormity of it all. His money tree was not simply rare. It was one of a kind. He was the only person in the world who had ever owned a money tree.

The only person in the world. He *was* different from everyone else. Wasn't this what people were always trying to prove in various ways? A person would search all his life for the one thing that distinguished him from everybody else. Some did crazy things, like crossing Death Valley on foot or eating eighty-five lemon meringue pies — just to show they could do something first, best, longest, most. Only a few people ever found that special something. But for Jason the search was over.

Never again would he need to wonder what he did best.

But how long would it be enough simply for *him* to know?

"Rejoice!" he told himself. "This is a very special gift. It's enough that *I* know and that I'm going to be rich."

But when they got home again and Jason went outside to check his money tree, he realized he wasn't going to be a millionaire quite as soon as he had thought. Six bills were unfurled, ready to fall, but not quite. They still felt damp and waxen to the touch. By morning he would harvest sixty more dollars. But the eight branches were not dividing as the others had done. Rather, several new shoots were forming near the base of the original stem.

Clearly, his harvest was not going to double every day. Nor would the bills proceed to mature in orderly fashion. There would be days of huge surprise, with a bumper crop, and days of growth without any harvest.

Jason felt rather relieved. He needed a rest, time to think. He must find some way to explain all this money to his parents. There was still the sweepstake idea, and it wouldn't be too hard to make his parents believe he'd won. He could probably fake an official letter, but how could he actually go about buying a house? How could he get away by himself even to find one? And, most troublesome of all, how could he be sure it was the right house? Would Mom and Dad really like it?

The very thought of this much responsibility made Jason feel weak. But now a new thought frightened him even more. Suppose that money tree never did stop producing. It might prosper for two hundred years, like the giant redwoods. What if it sent out new shoots, gave birth to a whole grove of money trees? Why, the money system of the whole world would be wrecked. Money, common as leaves, would have no value.

Jason ran to the bathroom, gulped a glass of water, and splashed his feverish cheeks. "Simmer down," he told himself. "Be reasonable. This money tree is like that whole ecology thing. If one person throws litter on the highway, it doesn't matter much. But if everybody did it..."

If everybody had a money tree, it would create a disaster. But there must be billions and trillions of dollars in the world. So what difference would one more little old million make?

His challenge was clear and he was strong, ready to meet it. The important thing was to keep his money tree under control. After all, he wasn't the only one ever to have discovered something new. If Columbus could adjust to the fact of a round world, if Ben Franklin could cope with his newly discovered electricity, then certainly he could handle a little old money tree growing in a pot.

Saturday, up early, Jason planned to mow the lawn before going to Mr. Matroni's. He went out right after breakfast, dragging the lawn mower behind him.

Dad, hearing the whir of the blades, poked his head out the window and called, "Glad to see you haven't forgotten about the lawn!"

Still looking back at Dad, Jason began to mow. He braced himself for a push against the uphill grade, and before he could stop the churning blades, he realized, in horror, that he had run right over two of the crisp, new ten-dollar bills. They lay on the grass, snipped into dozens of little pieces.

But that was not the worst. He could spare a couple of tens. Walking toward the flowerpot, Jason found another bill on the ground. But the other three had vanished.

On his hands and knees Jason crept over the entire lawn, hunting for them. Frantically, he searched under the two huge bushes and poked through the swirling dry leaves that always blew over from the Parkers' poplar tree. No luck.

Jason squatted down on the grass, chewing at his knuckles. From the corner of his eye he saw the large, waving pumpkin leaves in Mr. Quinley's garden. The pumpkin patch was Mr. Quinley's pride and joy. Every Halloween Mr. Quinley distributed pumpkins to all the neighborhood children. "I don't need them," he always said, "but I do like

to see them grow. Pumpkin blossoms are right pretty."

Now, at the far edge of Mr. Quinley's pumpkin patch, a strange-looking sprout was growing. Jason hung his body half over the fence, straining to see. Was it a weed? Oh, no. Another money tree was sprouting up right in the midst of Mr. Quinley's beloved pumpkin patch.

"I have two satisfactions in life," Mr. Quinley often said, "my pumpkins and my art." When he wasn't tending his pumpkins, Mr. Quinley hammered out pictures onto copper. Nobody ever bought his engravings. He didn't care. It gave him satisfaction.

With a burst of speed, Jason finished cutting the lawn, and cut grass flew around him like snow in a storm. As he mowed, he plotted. Then he ran next door.

Everybody's Bargain-Rate Gardener

"Come in! Door's open!" Bang-tap-a-tap, Mr. Quinley's hammer didn't lose a beat, and he barely glanced up as Jason entered. Then, without cracking a smile he murmured, "Who are you, the jolly green giant?"

In the hall mirror Jason got a glimpse of himself, green all over from grass cuttings, from his hair to his stockings.

"Good morning, Mr. Quinley," he said pleasantly.

"Selling something? Cookies, light bulbs, seeds, Christmas cards? We don't need any, thank you."

"No, sir. I — want to talk to you about — something else. That is, I think I lost my baseball in your backyard."

Mr. Quinley stood up. "I'll get it for you. I don't like to have people tramping on my pumpkin patch. It's just starting to fill in."

Jason had expected that. He was ready for the next round. "Actually, Mr. Quinley, I didn't see it *land* there. It must have landed in the Stoffers' yard."

"You want my permission to go into the Stoffers' yard?"

"Actually, I've got a business proposition, Mr. Quinley."

Mr. Quinley's eyebrows rose up into small black-winged shapes. "So?" He smiled as he polished his handiwork with a red flannel cloth. "Perhaps you are an art lover?" He gazed at the wall where dozens of engravings hung. "What can I do for you?"

"I thought," said Jason, "that I could do your weeding."

"My weeding? Don't you have any of your own?"

"Yes, sir, but I like to weed."

Mr. Quinley said nothing. He blew onto his engraving and continued to polish it with his cloth.

"See, I need to earn some money. My mom's birthday is coming up, and I want to buy her a present."

Mr. Quinley stopped polishing. His withered old face suddenly took on the glow of an eight-year-old who has just hit his first home run. And Jason knew there was only one way that he could get into Mr. Quinley's pumpkin patch.

"With the money I earn from weeding," he explained, "I will buy my mother one of your engravings."

The long silence and closed eyelids made Jason think maybe Mr. Quinley had passed out. "What do you think, sir? I'll only charge you fifty cents an hour. If you don't want to pay me cash, I'll work as many hours as it takes to pay for the engraving. While I'm weeding, you'll have time to work on the picture. What do you think, sir?"

"I think," said Mr. Quinley, "that if a boy wants to earn money to buy his mother a birthday present, a present of real value and lasting beauty, he should be encouraged. Yes, he should definitely be given a helping hand."

Jason grinned and held out his hand. They shook.

"I'll start right away," Jason said. "And I'll be very careful of your pumpkins. I'll come twice a week, if that's O.K."

"That's fine." Mr. Quinley stood up and led Jason toward his collection of engravings. "Which one," he asked, "did you have in mind?"

Jason gazed at the engravings. They were all alike in one respect. Geese. Geese flying in groups of three, five, seven. One goose alone on a branch. Two geese swimming in a pond. He couldn't possibly choose a ready-made one. The whole point was to keep Mr. Quinley busy, out of the backyard.

"Well," said Jason shifting from foot to foot, "none of these. You see, my mom doesn't like geese."

Mr. Quinley's eyebrows shot up. He winced, as if he were in pain. "Doesn't like geese?"

"Well, not exactly. I don't mean she doesn't *like* them. I guess she does like them. But she's allergic to them. Yes, bad, bad allergy. Anything with feathers makes her sneeze."

"And you think even an engraving of a goose...?"

Jason nodded. "It might remind her of the real thing, you know, those feathers. Then she'd start sneezing and getting all choked up."

Mr. Quinley frowned and paced, hands locked behind his back. "What exactly did you have in mind, Jason? And how much are you planning to pay for this special, made-to-order engraving?"

"A mermaid," said Jason immediately. "I know she'd like that."

"A mermaid. And what did you think you'd be able to pay?"

"Ten dollars?"

"Ten dollars. Well, let's just say that you'll weed for me for twenty hours, say, two days a week, two hours each day, for five weeks."

"Yes, sir."

"And when will you need the engraving?"

"Very soon. The sooner the better. In fact, if you

could start on it right now... and please make it big, Mr. Quinley, as big as you can. If it costs more, I'll pay it. I've got some money saved. I work at Mr. Matroni's, too."

"At the rate you're going," remarked Mr. Quinley, "I guess you'll be a millionaire. But please bear in mind, Jason, my pumpkin patch is very dear to me." He sighed. "Very dear."

Jason ran home to telephone Mr. Matroni, to explain that he couldn't come in today.

"Sure, partner," Mr. Matroni said cheerfully. "Take the day off. Go fishing. Play ball. Have fun."

Some fun, Jason thought grimly as he picked his way carefully through the pumpkin patch. Some fun.

It was the wind, of course. During the night the wind had sent the ten-dollar bills flying into the Quinleys' yard. Landing in the fertile pumpkin patch, they quickly took root and sprouted.

Jason pulled out the sprout and stuffed it into his pocket. Even as he sighed over the waste, he shivered at the thought of what might have happened if those bills had blown all over town. Thank goodness he had been alert. Now all he had to do was to find the other two sprouts.

On his hands and knees Jason plowed through the pumpkin patch, covering the entire garden again and again. His back began to ache, and he groaned like Atlas, with the weight of the world on his back. Still he searched, all in vain. No money sprouts.

Wearily, Jason stood up and gazed down upon yard after yard, identically square and bounded by fences. His sprouts could be anywhere!

His throat tightened. How long before money trees started growing like wild flowers in gardens and on hillsides all over the state? The President of the United States in Washington, D.C., would announce on TV, "My fellow Americans, we are caught in a national disaster. Our money is not even worth the paper it's printed on. All over this nation, money is growing on trees."

Then the IRS, the FBI, the National Guard, and all sorts of officers in uniform would descend upon Silverview. Quickly, they would trace the original money tree to Jason Galloway. Screaming headlines would accuse him, BOY GROWS MONEY TREE, CAUSES CRISIS.

From the street Jason heard the shouts of little kids playing baseball. Oh, to be out there with no worries, catching flies, running bases!

"Run! Hide! Destroy the money tree!" His own advice flew at him, leaving Jason unable to choose or even to move. Then came another echo. "Be reasonable!" Yes, reasonable. The wind blew from west to east. The bills could only have blown eastward. He must proceed to attack his problem in an orderly way.

Jason forced a lift to his shoulders. He urged a

bounce into his step. He put on a happy face, then walked next door to the Stoffers' and rang the bell.

"Mrs. Stoffer, I've got a business proposition for you..."

After laboring for over an hour through the Stoffers' disgraceful mass of weeds, Jason found one more of his missing sprouts. But where was the third sprout? As Jason stood up, he stifled a cry. There, way down in the MacKenzies' yard, between two huge cacti and a bunch of geraniums — there it was.

Gathering the last of his strength, Jason dragged himself to the MacKenzies' door.

"Fifty cents an hour!" exclaimed fat, puffing Mrs. MacKenzie. "My, that's a bargain. I should say you may weed my yard. In fact, I'll hire you to come twice a week."

It was incredible, absurd. He ought to be famous, with his picture on the covers of national magazines. Instead, he had become everybody's bargain-rate gardener. He owned a thriving money tree, yet he'd never worked harder in his life. True, he had earned four dollars and seventy-five cents. The neighbors all praised his work and wanted him regularly. But he hated gardening. Angrily, he called himself names. "Stupid! Careless! Idiot!" What he needed was a proper routine. And he needed a money-tree money-catcher.

All Sunday Jason pondered his problem. Twelve

new buds had emerged; fortunately, they were still small. He needed time to think.

Sunday night Jason had a brilliant idea. He would use the old beach umbrella in the garage. They never went to the beach anyhow. Nobody would miss it.

On Monday, after working at Matroni's, Jason got a large carton from the supermarket.

On Tuesday morning, Jason put the flowerpot inside the carton and covered it with the beach umbrella, thereby creating the first original money-tree money-catcher. To celebrate his success, Jason decided to go to Matroni's and buy himself the Super-Duper pole.

"I sold it this morning," Mr. Matroni said regretfully. "But I'll be getting in more. I'll save one for you."

"It figures," muttered Jason. He could picture that skinny poltergeist sitting on the roof, laughing his head off.

On Wednesday, when Jason went to check his money tree with the ingenious new catcher, he clutched at his stomach, sickened and horrified. Like dried-out pea pods left hanging too long on the vine, his precious money buds were shriveled and brown.

Furiously, Jason hurled the umbrella across the yard. He bent down as if to embrace the poor plant. "I'm sorry," he wept, and his tears slid down into the dry, hard soil. "I took away all your sun, air, and moisture. I'm so *sorry*! I'm supposed to be smart. Then why am I so stupid?"

Gently, Jason watered the plant. "Get well," he pleaded, "and I'll buy you a new, big, comfortable pot."

All night Jason tossed in his sleep, dreaming of marvelous inventions. Unfortunately, none of them applied to catching a money-tree harvest. But by morning, the money tree had made a miraculous recovery. What might have caused it? "Tears," Jason gasped. "*My tears.*"

Suddenly, Mr. Quinley's voice and Mr. Quinley's shadow fell over Jason, making him squat down in a hurry. "Jason, I need you to come and weed today. If you want me to devote my time to that mermaid..."

"Coming, Mr. Quinley."

Weed for Mr. Quinley, watch the buds, make a catcher, go to the store and buy a flowerpot — the day simply wasn't long enough.

Jason raced to the telephone. "Mr. Matroni, I can't come in today. I've — got chores to do at home."

After a slight pause came a faint sigh. "All right, partner. See you Saturday?"

"Saturday for sure," Jason replied. "I'm sorry."

As Jason finished Mr. Quinley's weeding, the great idea struck. It was born of two causes. He heard Mrs. Stoffer's wheezy singing, "I'm only a bird in a gilded cage." And he saw an old roll of chicken wire in Mr. Quinley's garage. What he needed was not a catcher, but a cage.

It was wonderfully easy to talk Mr. Quinley out of that chicken wire. To an artist like Mr. Quinley, the magic word was "creative."

"Mr. Quinley," said Jason, "if only I had some chicken wire, I could start that creative art project I've been wanting to try."

With the chicken wire, an old mop handle, and several croquet wickets, Jason fashioned a kind of wire tepee, which he placed gently over the money tree. It was not a thing of beauty. "But neither is a safety pin," thought Jason. "The important thing is that it works."

Deeply satisfied, Jason sat down beside his creation and crooned a lullabye.

"Sleep, my child, and peace attend thee
All through the night."

So sweet was the song, so great Jason's relief, that he managed to work up two or three tender tears. These he carefully let fall into the flowerpot. Before his eyes, one by one, the twelve bills dropped down from their stems and were safely contained inside his tepee. Gleefully, Jason lifted the wire, took out his harvest, ran inside. Now twenty-one ten-dollar bills lay in the silver box.

They seemed too crisp and lovely to spend. So

Jason reached into the jar where he kept his ordinary money, and took five dollars, and set out to buy a new flowerpot.

It was only three o'clock, two hours before the stores closed. He'd drop in on Mr. Matroni, maybe help him with the new deliveries that always came on Thursdays.

As Jason entered Matroni's, the little bell tinkled in welcome. But the store was empty and oddly quiet. Several boxes of tennis socks lay on the floor, as if they'd been knocked down by someone in a hurry.

"Mr. Matroni!" Jason called. "Mr. Matroni!" He moved further into the store. Then he heard a desperate thumping and shouting.

"Let me out! Let me out!"

Jason ran back to the record booth. Two heavy desk chairs had been jammed against the door. From within came the choked shouts, "In here! Locked in!"

"Just a minute, Mr. Matroni," Jason yelled. He struggled to remove the chair that had been braced under the doorknob. At last Mr. Matroni emerged, red-faced and breathless.

"They pushed me in and barricaded the door. Thieves! They must have been after..."

They rushed to the cash register. Mr. Matroni pushed the "No Sale" key, and the drawer flew open. It was empty.

The Finger of Suspicion

Mr. Matroni seemed about to collapse. Red-faced, trembling, he tugged at his hair, moaning, "Oh! Oh! Would you believe it? Never, never in all my life — and they were such nice-looking kids, three of them. Clean *nice-looking kids!*"

Mr. Matroni sank down on a chair and mopped his face. "If you hadn't come along, partner.... If only I'd taken the money to the bank."

"How much did they steal?" Jason asked.

"I know exactly because I was just getting ready to make a deposit. I'd just counted it. One hundred and seventy-two dollars and forty-eight cents. Oh, I'll have to call the sheriff right away."

While they waited for the sheriff, Mr. Matroni

told the whole sad story. "I had just finished counting the money. I was late — what a day I had! All the kids came in for baseballs — must have heard about the new shipment. Between unpacking the new merchandise and waiting on customers, I was rushing all day. By the time I'd finished counting the money, it was too late to go to the bank."

With every word Jason sank deeper into despair. If he'd been here, Mr. Matroni would have sent him to the bank with the money. The robbery would never have occurred.

"Things quieted down then," Mr. Matroni continued. "Only three teen-agers were left, two boys and a girl. The girl asked me to put on a record for her. I went in to the booth with her. Next thing I knew she'd slammed the door on me. They pulled up those chairs, then cleaned out my cash register." Mr. Matroni was so distressed that he mopped his face with the dustcloth he always kept in his back pocket. "If you hadn't come along, Jason...you saved the day."

"If I had been here," Jason whispered, "it wouldn't have happened. It was my fault."

"Now, don't blame yourself, partner. It was just one of those things."

The bell tinkled; the sheriff strode into the store. "Another robbery!" he grumbled accusingly. Obviously, he took crime as a personal insult.

Tall and puffy-cheeked, the sheriff mumbled

through half-closed lips. His eyes, too, were half closed and constantly shifting. He took out a note pad and looked down coolly at Mr. Matroni.

"What happened?"

When Mr. Matroni had finished his story, the sheriff asked stiffly, "Do you usually keep this much cash in the store?"

"No. As I told you, I didn't have a chance to get to the bank."

"Are you usually alone in the store?" The sheriff's eyes shifted toward Jason.

"No — well, not always. This is my partner, Jason Galloway. That is, I call him my partner." Mr. Matroni gave Jason a fond smile. "He comes in to help me two or three days a week."

"Regular days?"

"Usually Monday, Thursday, and Saturday. But today he was busy."

"I see. Busy." The sheriff's mouth worked over the word as he studied Jason from head to toe. "But wasn't it you," he asked, "who let Mr. Matroni out of the booth?"

Jason nodded.

Abruptly, the sheriff turned to Mr. Matroni. "Could you identify the youngsters who locked you in the booth?"

Jason noted, with a cold feeling along his spine, that the sheriff had not said, "the youngsters who robbed you."

"Oh, yes, I think so," replied Mr. Matroni.

"They seemed like such nice kids. Clean — with shoes. Neat — no hair."

"Bald, you say?" asked the sheriff, pencil poised.

"No, not bald. I mean short hair, not wild or bushy. They were nice, clean-looking kids!"

"Have you seen them in this neighborhood before?"

"No, never."

"And you don't have an alarm system in the store?"

"No."

"But of course, you're insured..."

"No."

"What was that exact amount again?"

"One hundred and seventy-two dollars."

Jason chimed in, "And forty-eight cents!"

"That's right," agreed Mr. Matroni. "My partner here's got a good memory."

"Since you've got such a good memory," the sheriff said to Jason, "would you mind telling me what you did today?"

Weakly Jason replied. "I did some weeding for my neighbor. Then I had lunch."

"Was anyone with you?"

"Of course! My parents."

"That's fine, Jason. I'll need your full name and address for the statement. Please sign here, Mr. Matroni. We'll get to the bottom of this."

For a long moment he regarded Jason with a

fixed stare, then walked stiffly to the door. Jason watched him, anticipating that last remark, the warning always given to a person under suspicion. "Don't plan on leaving town for a few days."

Having reached the door, the sheriff paused. He turned. His eyes fastened on Jason. He said, "Good-bye."

But that didn't prove anything. It only showed that the sheriff was clever, thought Jason. He was too smart to alert Jason to the fact that the finger of suspicion was pointed right at *him.*

The moment Jason entered the living room, his mother cried out, "Jason, what's wrong?"

With great effort he controlled his breathing and brought his voice to a steady tone. As he told about the robbery, his own voice seemed distant and unbelievably calm. Only part of him, it seemed, was here in this shadowy present telling the tale. The other part of him was knotted with a fear too deep to express, but it throbbed inside him like a hammer beat. The finger of suspicion was pointing at *him.*

Jason told it all, then retold it to his dad. They made the usual comments, "Oh, dear, that's a shame. I know how you feel." But how could they know? Abruptly, Dad went back to his books, and Mom told Jason to empty the garbage and set the table, as if nothing important had really happened.

Fear made him meek, made him obey when his mother shouted, "Jason! See what Dinah's doing. She was here a minute ago. Hurry!"

Jason hurried down the hall. In the bathroom stood Dinah, bent over the toilet bowl. Jason pounced at her with a shout. "Dinah! What did you do?"

"Bye-bye," the baby cooed, clapping her hands. "Bye-bye."

The water swirled round and round. On the top floated Mom's good box of dusting powder and a fluffy red powder puff.

"Boat!" shrieked Dinah.

Roughly, Jason picked her up and gave her a shake. "Bad, bad girl," he shouted. "Shame on you." Angrily, he carried her into the living room, put her down in the playpen, and she began to wail.

"Don't be so angry with her," Mom said. "She didn't know better."

Still, Jason felt furious, and he banged the door to his room. Never before had he been so angry at Dinah. Angry at the baby? No — Jason knew that his anger really had nothing to do with Dinah. He had failed Mr. Matroni. He had lied. He had plotted and schemed, and now he was going to pay the price.

Oh, he knew exactly what that sheriff was thinking, building up a case against him. How come

Jason happened to be in the store so soon after the robbery? Why, if he was too busy to work today, did he show up just in time to save Mr. Matroni? How did he know exactly how much money was missing?

The sheriff had not searched him. So what? That only proved he didn't have a search warrant with him. And Jason couldn't forget that question: "Could you identify the youngsters who locked you in the booth?"

Clearly, the sheriff's keen mind envisioned two separate crimes. He might think Jason was in cahoots with those three clean teen-agers. Or that the teen-agers had locked Mr. Matroni in the booth only as a prank. Then Jason had come along and seized the opportunity to rob his employer.

From the kitchen Jason heard his parents talking about him.

"He's been so edgy lately..."

"Gardening all over the neighborhood..."

"Trying to earn money for your birthday present, Liz."

"Good kid, he's taking this so hard."

"He feels a great loyalty to Mr. Matroni."

The sight of his own face in the mirror disgusted Jason. He hadn't given a single thought to poor Mr. Matroni, with four kids to support and no insurance. He had only thought about himself. What a partner! What a pal!

Late that night Mom came in and sat down on Jason's bed. It wasn't his fault, she said. He was a good worker, a faithful friend to Mr. Matroni. "Don't worry about it anymore."

"The sheriff took my name and address," Jason said.

"That's just routine. You're a witness."

"He might come and talk to you."

"Let him come! I'll be glad to talk to him."

Jason couldn't tell whether he was sleeping and dreaming or awake and worrying. Either way, the same nightmare tormented him. The sheriff would come to the house. His parents would swear that Jason had been home until three that afternoon.

"But you don't know exactly what Jason did after that, do you? You don't know what actually happened in Matroni's store when Jason first walked in and found the place empty. You don't really know how tempted he would be by the sight of all that money."

"Well, he does send for lots of things free..."

"He's a good boy!" Mom cries.

"Then you won't mind, Mrs. Galloway, if I search his room."

"I know my legal rights!" shouts Dad. "You can't search without a warrant."

"I happen to have a search warrant right here in my pocket."

The sheriff searches and finds the ten-dollar

bills in the silver box. "Jason Galloway, can you explain this?"

"I have a money tree in the backyard."

"Sure, kid. You'll have to come downtown with me."

"Just look! I'll prove it."

"Quit stalling, kid. Of all the crazy alibis..."

"Dad! Come out in the yard with me. It's not a snail. It's a money tree."

"Sorry, son. I've got to study for the bar exam."

"Mom! You come and look."

"Sorry, Jason. I'm working on my Dream House scrapbook."

In loud, chilling tones the sheriff says, "Jason Galloway, I wish to inform you of your legal rights. I must warn you that anything you say may be used against you."

Jason sat up with a start. His sheets felt clammy against his skin. Outside a cat yeowled — or was it a poltergeist shrieking with fiendish pleasure at Jason's fears?

That sheriff would hang onto this case like a bulldog. He wouldn't give up until Mr. Matroni's money was found. There was only one way out. It involved a terrible risk, but he'd have to chance it.

Jason's problems sprouted like mushrooms. Everybody was after him. The sheriff, the neighbors, even Dad, who with only three days left before the bar exam was acting most peculiar. He ran to his books in the midst of shaving, leaving pasty foam to thicken on his cheeks. He ate hundreds of raisins for extra energy. He absentmindedly peppered his eggs until they were black, then swore he was catching a terrible cold when the pepper caused violent sneezing.

"Take it easy, Jonathan," Mom said soothingly. "You've got to relax. I've called Aunt Tilda to stay with the kids on Sunday, and we'll go out. You've got to *relax*."

The prospect of spending a whole day with Aunt Tilda made Jason shudder with dread. Equally disturbing was the phrase he had heard Dad mumbling last night over his studies. "Congress shall have the sole power to coin money." Sole power — only power. With a sinking feeling Jason wondered whether a man could become a lawyer if his son was a criminal. All these lonely years, long evenings, thousands of facts crammed into Dad's tired brain — for nothing.

It was midmorning, but Jason huddled in his bed, counting his problems. He wished for something definite, an attack of acute appendicitis, a festering molar, or a good throat infection, anything to ease the mental pain of remembering, Mr. Matroni's kids without their milk money; the hounding sheriff; the shrieking neighbors screaming over fences, "Jason! Come and weed today!";

the drumming question in his mind, "Is it legal?"

Mom came in to ask anxiously, "Jason, are you sick?"

He almost moaned, picturing the dainty foods and sweet comfort she would give. But then he remembered. He had to get up, tend the money tree, work out his plot to get the sheriff off his trail.

"I'm fine!" He leaped up. "Fit as a fiddle!"

"Well, be very quiet today."

"I'll stay outside — with my snail."

Out, out to see his beautiful money tree — yes, that would soothe him. But even the birds had joined the conspiracy. Perched atop the wire cage was a fat black bird greedily pecking holes into a juicy ten-dollar bill.

"Scat!" Jason screamed, throwing a rock at the bird. Several bees buzzed by with evil intentions. No doubt they sought some delicious new nectar from his money-tree buds. They would proceed to cover the earth with money-tree pollen. Then, what strange hybrids might appear? Perhaps a cross between a ten-dollar bill and an apple? Would it be edible?

The black bird screeched from the Parkers' poplar tree. Furious, Jason flung another rock. It hit the side of the Parkers' house, and a head appeared at the window almost immediately.

"Guess what?"

"What?" Jason shouted back.

"You almost broke our window."

"Well, I didn't, did I?"

"Want to go fishing at Lake Serra?"

Oh yes, fishing at Lake Serra, even fishing in that slimy hole with auto exhaust poisoning the surrounding air. Yes, he would give anything to be fishing for socks in Lake Serra at this very moment.

"I can't, Dave. I've promised to weed for Mrs. Stoffer today."

"Gee, you can never do anything anymore. Hey, what's that funny-looking thing?"

"I am growing a rare plant. A Venus's-flytrap. It eats people who don't mind their own business. For dinner."

"Gee, Jason, I think you are making fun of me."

In the next moment Dave was gone. "There goes my only friend," thought Jason sorrowfully. Well, who needs friends? Once he had his pockets full of money, he'd have plenty of friends, and plenty of fun. And the money tree was budding like crazy, sending out new shoots, making new buds on every branch. He would buy a new pot for it right away, then maybe have time to go to Lake Serra.

He ran to the store and returned with a large new flowerpot. His hands were shaking from hurrying so, and he struggled to compose himself. He must rid himself of all anxiety and anger, for plants could sense ill will. He had read about that. Bad thoughts could put a plant into shock.

"I am very happy," Jason whispered, as gently he lifted the plant from its pot. "I love everybody, especially plants."

Singing "My Country 'Tis of Thee," Jason transplanted his tree. It spread its branches, settling itself into the new pot, and seven bills fluttered down like pale green butterflies. Sixteen buds waited for harvesting tomorrow. For a brief moment Jason felt the ectasy of accomplishment. Then came a shriek across the fence.

"Jaa-son! Aren't you going to weed for me today?"

"Coming, Mrs. Stoffer!"

Jason ran to put his bills away, ran out again to Mrs. Stoffer's. He felt like a trained seal, ready to flap like a fool at everyone's beck and call. Let the silver box bulge; let the harvest rain down. He hadn't spent any of it, not a penny. He didn't have time.

More Stately Mansions

While Jason was gone, the mail had come, with a letter and a package from the Town House Country House Sweepstake. "The letter was addressed to J. Galloway," Mom said, as in one instant Jason's hopes soared, then sank. "Dad opened it by mistake."

"Did he read it?" Jason cried.

"Shh. I told you, it was a mistake."

Gone, gone was his last hope for buying a dream house on the sly, for now he could never fake a letter saying he had won it. Numb with despair, Jason read the letter.

Dear Mr. Galloway,
   We are happy to inform you that while your number did not win first prize in our sweepstake,

> we are sending you a consolation prize of our
> beautiful gardening guide, volume I. Additional
> volumes of this set may be purchased at the un-
> usual price of $5.95 each.

That crazy book! He wanted to throw it out the window. Didn't they know he *hated* gardening?

The phone rang. Jason crossed his fingers. Let it be good news!

"Jason, Mrs. MacKenzie wants you to come over and weed now."

Late that afternoon when Dad asked, "Want to go out and hit a few baseballs?" Jason could only shake his head miserably. Every bone in his body rebelled against those hours of bending. Bees in Mrs. MacKenzie's pyracantha bushes had gone on a rampage. Three stings on his arms were swollen, red, and painful.

Jason sighed. "I'm sorry, Dad. I'm just too tired."

"Seems to me you've been overdoing it, son. Why don't you go out and play tomorrow?"

"I have to go to Mr. Matroni's tomorrow. I earned $3.75 today, Dad!"

"Jason, why all this sudden desire for money? You're exhausted, working every minute."

Jason kept his eyes down. "I don't know." How could he talk to Dad, with so many things between them that must remain secret?

"Jason, I only..."

"Leave me alone, Dad!"

In the next moment Dad was gone, and Jason felt the ache of his muscles spreading inside him. What good is a secret if nobody knows it? What fun is it to make miracles when nobody cares? How great it would be to carry that thick wad of money in his pocket and take in the admiring glances of friends, neighbors, even strangers. No wonder rich people like Aunt Tilda lived in mansions and rode around in sleek, expensive cars. Because when you're rich, people think you're very smart and important.

A sudden memory of Grandpa brought a pang of guilt. Grandpa, with hardly ever more than a dollar in his pocket, was without a doubt the wisest person Jason had ever known.

From the silver box Jason counted out one hundred and seventy dollars in tens. These he put into an envelope. He took two dollars and forty-eight cents in change from the jar. Now at least one of his problems would be solved.

About to set off for work, Jason remembered the demands of his money tree. He watered it and gathered in a bumper crop of sixteen new bills. Strange — those first bills had filled him with shivers of excitement and sparkling dreams. Now it had become almost routine.

Three black birds sat ominously still on the telephone wire, spying, probably plotting to peck his bills full of holes. Jason clenched his teeth and made a fist. All right! He'd show them. He'd make a scarecrow. He'd show them all! His was the greatest talent in the world. The law is made for ordinary people doing ordinary things. There *is* no law against miracles. Did a volcano, before it spouted, need to get a burning permit? Ridiculous! And when a magician pulls a rabbit out of a hat, does he have to pay a tax on it? Of course not.

Jason stuffed the sixteen new bills into the silver box. He would wait until he had a full million; then nobody would deny the miracle, then power would raise him above the common man, even above the law. For now, he must only remain cautious. What's so hard about making a scarecrow? He had to keep his wits about him.

Dad suddenly appeared in the doorway, and Jason clapped the lid on the silver box. "You always ask *me* to knock first," he complained.

"I'm sorry, son." Dad's smile faded into a look of hurt astonishment. "I'm sorry," he repeated. "I thought that if you're going to work, you'd pick up some more raisins for me."

"Sure," Jason murmured, filled with shame and regret. All Dad wanted was raisins for energy to pass the bar exam. And why? So he could go to court and defend the poor, uphold the law, bring justice.

"Son, what's worrying you?" Dad put his arm around Jason's shoulder and drew him close. "Have I been fussing at you too much? It'll soon be over."

"I'm O.K." Jason drew away. Dad's closeness, the comfort of his arms, would make him cry. Then he'd have to reveal it all, confess about the money tree and all his troubles. He'd have to take Dad out into the yard, and even as they approached, the money tree would wither and die. And then who would ever believe him? Nobody in his right mind would doubt that Jason had stolen Mr. Matroni's money. And worse, Jason would be blamed for every robbery that had taken place in the entire county, with those ten-dollar bills in the silver box as evidence.

"I'd better be going, Dad," Jason said.

Of course, he couldn't just go up to Mr. Matroni and hand him the money. He had to replace it secretly. If he got caught returning the money, anybody would assume he had stolen it to begin with — even Mr. Matroni himself.

If only he could go to the bank and change those tens for some larger bills. But the bank was closed on Saturdays. Anyhow, it would look suspicious for a boy like him to come in with a wad of tens.

On Saturdays Mr. Matroni always counted up the day's earnings before he closed the store. Then he would take the money home for safekeeping over the weekend. He would deposit it as soon as the bank opened on Monday morning.

All day Jason thought only of closing time. He needed just a few minutes, with Mr. Matroni out of sight.

Finally it was five o'clock. Mr. Matroni counted the day's receipts, put the money in his pocket, and said, as always, "Closing time." Then, "Did you turn out the lights in the back room?"

Pretending to be very busy working a knot out of his shoelace, Jason said, "No. I forgot."

Mr. Matroni's brows rose in surprise. "I'll go do it," he said.

The instant Mr. Matroni was out of sight, Jason let out a burst of song, the first song that came to his mind.

"I wanna hold your hand!" he sang loudly. At the same time he struck the "No Sale" key, singing over the sound of the cash register bell. "I wanna hold your hand! Yeah, yeah, yeah, yeah!"

Quickly, Jason slipped his bills far into the cash drawer and banged it shut with another "Yeah, yeah, yeah, yeah!"

"Well, you're in a good mood," Mr. Matroni remarked as he locked the front door. "Come on, I'll drive you home."

Jason suppressed a grin. Everything was going to be all right. "Yeah! Yeah! Yeah! Yeah!" he sang, feeling free and very virtuous.

Jason had overslept. He awakened to the rude sound of Aunt Tilda's dry, cackling laughter. "Oh, the children and I will have a fine time. You and Jonathan go along. Don't worry about a thing."

Mom rushed in. "Hurry, Jason. Aunt Tilda's waiting for you." Seeing his expression, she added, "It won't be so bad, Jason. Aunt Tilda's going to take you out. You'll have fun. And when we get home, maybe we'll have a surprise for you."

No possible surprise could make up for Aunt Tilda's sudden appearance in his room, her pointing finger. "Young man, you are keeping us waiting!"

Jason gulped a hasty breakfast to the accompaniment of Aunt Tilda's senseless chatter. "Now big brother is eating his grapefruit. See, Dinah, how brother holds his spoon?"

Dinah threw her hard-boiled egg across the room.

"Brother does not throw his egg, Dinah. See big brother eating his egg?"

By the time they were settled in Aunt Tilda's car, Jason felt that he was already drowning in words. "See? Big brother is putting on his seat belt, just like an astronaut."

Aunt Tilda decided that what Jason and baby Dinah needed was culture. She set her long black car in motion. They sped right past the zoo.

"Culture," said Aunt Tilda with a sniff, "is *not* watching a tribe of naked monkeys doing foolish tricks in cages."

They drove past the aquarium, and Aunt Tilda said, "Culture is *not* watching the fish playing tag in a tank."

Jason only sighed as they drove past the Japanese Tea Garden with its cool wispy ferns and green willows. Even Dinah was strangely subdued. She sucked her thumb and rolled her eyes as if to say, "All right. You win. I'll take my medicine."

Culture, it turned out, meant going straight to a musty gray building downtown. It meant sitting on hard chairs and listening to a gray-haired, gray-gowned woman playing the harpsichord. Afterward, it meant listening to Aunt Tilda deliver a long lecture about the merits of the harpsichord, "an honorable instrument, refined and delicate, soothing to the senses."

They wandered in and out of antique shops on Union Street, and Jason envied the dogs that lolled in the gutter. Dinah in her stroller had fallen into a deep and merciful sleep.

They drove along the quiet, tree-lined streets of Pacific Heights, where large, elegant mansions stood beyond vast lawns and black iron gates.

"Here's your house!" Jason said suddenly. Aunt Tilda slowed the car. She parked across the street from the great stone lions that squatted beside the twin pillars of the porch. Beyond the gleaming black door, Jason knew, lay fleecy white carpets, chairs and sofas of rich blue velvet, everything matching, gleaming, perfect as a magazine picture.

"Are we going to your house?" Jason asked. Inside Aunt Tilda's house he always felt too clumsy, too dirty, too rough.

"No," said Aunt Tilda, blinking her eyes rapidly. "That is not my house anymore. I've moved to an apartment."

"You have!"

Aunt Tilda threw back her head and quoted, "Build thee more stately mansions, O my soul!"

Inwardly, Jason groaned. He was ignorant of poetry, and he wanted to keep it that way. But curiosity overcame him. "What do you mean?" he asked.

Aunt Tilda turned to face him. "Last year," she began, "I realized that the house was too much for me. I had always loved it, as you know. But" — she sighed — "the silver alone took an entire morning to polish. Oh, I had a maid, of course, but one must attend to so many things. After my husband passed away, I began to feel as if — the house was owning *me*. Things! Things! Carpets to protect, windows to wash, bric-a-brac to dust. Things! They were owning me.

"So I decided," she said, "that I must build myself a different kind of mansion." She quoted again. "'Build thee more stately mansions, O my soul!' Do you understand, Jason? When a person gets to be my age, the days fly. What had I done with them except to collect *things*? But I loved that house. I didn't want to see it go. I hoped to keep it in the family. I have nobody, as you know, except for your mother. No other blood kin. But your mother didn't — she wouldn't — she didn't want my mansion."

"You wanted to give it to us?" Jason exclaimed.

"I — offered your parents a suitable arrangement," said Aunt Tilda briskly. "I love my niece," she continued, "but you might as well know it; your mother is the most stubborn woman who ever walked this earth. She refused my offer. She thanked me quite politely, but she refused. She said — how did she put it? She said that a dream house is a very personal thing. A dream house, she said, isn't any good unless you put it together yourself, bit by bit."

Jason sat dumbfounded. He remembered that house, a true dream house if there ever was one. And Mom didn't want it!

A very personal thing. Yes, a dream house, any dream, is a very *personal* thing.

Dazed and weary, Jason was only half aware of the restaurant where Aunt Tilda took them to dinner. Mechanically, he ate, working his way through the masses of food that kept appearing on his plate. Hazily he heard Aunt Tilda's chatter, "My, big brother has a good appetite."

On the way home he fell asleep in the car. Still groggy, he climbed into bed. Briefly, he remembered something about a surprise. He wanted only his warm covers, a soft pillow. He'd had enough surprises.

Very early Jason heard Dad clattering about. "Good luck on the bar exam!" he wanted to call, but then he heard the door slam, and Dad was gone. Taking that bar exam, Jason thought suddenly, is a very personal thing, a kind of battle that one fights all alone.

Mom seemed unusually cheerful as she fixed Jason's breakfast, although thick fog crept around the windows.

"I thought fog depresses you," Jason remarked.

"Not today," Mom smiled.

"Aren't you worried about Dad taking the exam?"

"No. This is his big day. I'm happy for him."

Jason nodded. "I know what you mean."

"Yes," Mom said, smiling. "I think you do."

With a start Jason remembered his money tree. Aunt Tilda and her culture had erased it from his mind all day yesterday. He gulped down the rest of his breakfast, determined to go right out and water it. But the telephone rang. It was Mr. Matroni, yelling into the phone excitedly, "Jason! Can you come over right away? Hurry!"

Jason hurried into his clothes and ran all the way to the shopping center. Mr. Matroni stood at the door waiting for him.

"It came back!" he cried, gleefully tugging at his hair. "My money, one hundred and seventy-two dollars and forty-eight cents! It's all here."

Jason grinned. "That's great, Mr. Matroni."

"Great!" Mr. Matroni agreed. "But, Jason, something strange — it's all in tens. Except for the two dollars and forty-eight cents, of course. Why would those kids have robbed me and then paid me back in tens?"

"Maybe so your money couldn't be identified?" Jason guessed.

"Maybe. I guess they felt guilty, had a change of heart. I told you they were nice, clean-looking kids. But how did they get in?"

"Maybe with a pass key," Jason offered.

"Could be. But, Jason, I have looked at those bills very carefully. And it's queer — they're all exactly in order."

"What do you mean, Mr. Matroni?"

"Look for yourself. Here. The serial numbers are all in a straight series: 769203, 769204, 769205. Why would they have bothered to get seventeen bills all numbered in succession?"

Jason chuckled. That good old money tree of his sure thought of everything! No two serial numbers were alike.

Suddenly, Mr. Matroni let out a gleeful yelp. "Hey! What do I care about the numbers? I've got my money back."

"That's all that matters," said Jason.

111

First Mr. Matroni called his wife, then the sheriff. "The sheriff says this kind of thing has happened before," he told Jason. "Sometimes kids get a guilty conscience and return the money. Kids!" he said vehemently. "Kids nowadays don't know what it's like to do a decent day's work, earn a respectable dollar. They talk a lot about love, but do they really care about other people's feelings? They all want something for nothing."

Suddenly, Mr. Matroni clapped Jason on the back. "Well, well," he said, "listen to me, talking crazy. Because here *you* are, my partner. Terrific!"

The Poltergeist Strikes Again

As he was walking home, Jason saw his dad drive by and ran to catch up with him at the corner. "How was it?" he asked. "Was it hard? Did you pass?"

"Yes, it was very hard. But, Jason, I knew the answers! I think I passed. I won't know for sure until September."

"September!" Jason cried.

"It takes a long time to grade those exams. And I only took the first part today. I've got two more parts to take."

"I thought you'd be finished! You said after the exam...Dad, I don't want to have to wait two more months!"

"The waiting's nearly over, Jason," Dad said gently. "But then, there are always other things to wait for and work for."

They arrived at the house, and Mom ran out to meet them. "Jason!" she said sharply. "Go inside and watch Dinah. She's been getting into everything. Hurry!"

Jason hung back, scowling. His parents stood close together, talking softly.

"Go on!" Mom called sternly.

Jason found Dinah sitting quietly on the kitchen floor playing with the canned goods. He wondered what his parents were talking about. He hated it when they huddled together like that, telling secrets. The telephone rang, and before he could answer it, his mother had dashed inside and grabbed the receiver from him.

When she had finished, she turned to Dad. "Nothing," she said with a strange look. "It was only a wrong number."

"Tomorrow?"

"I guess so," Mom replied.

"What's going on?" Jason demanded angrily. "Why won't you tell me?"

His parents gazed at each other, their eyes asking the question. Mom nodded slightly, smiling.

Dad turned to Jason and said, "Yesterday your mother and I drove to Mill Valley. It's across the bay, you know, in Marin County. It's really a fine town. Your mother and I have been considering moving there. Actually, we've wanted to live there for quite some time. But it was impossible while I was going to law school. Between working and my classes, I wouldn't have been able to come home for dinner at night. I wouldn't have been able to see you. But now..."

Jason held his breath.

"Yesterday," Dad continued, "we made an offer on a house in Mill Valley. It's a big old house with eight large rooms and a veranda."

"It's on nearly two acres of land!" Mom burst in, her eyes glowing. "There's a whole forest out back, huge oaks..."

"And the school is just down the hill," Dad added.

"The weather was so beautiful!" Mom exclaimed. "It's hard to believe it's only half an hour from Silverview. We drove right out of the fog into the sunshine. It was like another world. And, Jason, the house has a big basement. We'd have to fix it up a bit, a few coats of paint, shelves for our books..."

"We weren't going to tell you yet," Dad explained. "We're waiting for a call from the realtor, to see whether our offer has been accepted."

It was too sudden. Before he realized it, Jason was holding tight to Dad and crying.

Dad held him, patted his shoulder, then said

gruffly, "Come on now. I'm going to need your help. Right after dinner I want you to quiz me on my notes for tomorrow."

For hours, it seemed, Dad rolled off fact after fact from the study notes. "I don't see how you learned all that," Jason said sleepily when they were finished.

"Patience," Dad replied. "Now, you'd better get to bed."

Patience! The word burst into his brain, reminding him of the gold watch, then of the money tree. He hadn't watered it in two days! Lightly Jason tiptoed down the hall, determined to tend to it immediately.

"Hey!" Dad caught him by the arm. "Where do you think you're going? It's after ten."

"But Dad..."

"No buts. Go to bed."

In bed, Jason worried. He'd have to stay awake and sneak out later. But he felt strangely limp and very relaxed. Well, it had been very damp and foggy out. He would wait till morning. By morning a huge harvest would be waiting for him inside the wire cage. First thing in the morning he'd run outside...

First thing in the morning the phone jarred him awake. Next thing, Mom came bursting into his room. "The house! It's ours! They've accepted our offer. Tell you what, let's drive out there, you and

Dinah and I. I can't wait to see it again, to have you see it!"

They rushed through breakfast. As they drove through the city and over the Golden Gate Bridge, Jason kept telling himself that it was probably a horrible old house. The two acres were probably covered with rattlesnakes and poison oak. No doubt the house was high on a hill, with no kids around and no place to ride a bike. Inside it probably smelled of mildew, as old houses often do.

They turned off the highway at the sign "Mill Valley" and drove along tree-shaded streets where children played in summer clothes, running barefoot. Jason pulled off his jacket.

"Nice and warm, isn't it?" Mom crooned happily.

"Where's our house?" Jason asked suspiciously.

"You'll see."

They drove past a large quiet pond, past a baseball field where half a dozen boys were playing. They turned up a gentle hill. Several squirrels darted between the branches of trees. A dog trotted by, followed by a boy on a bicycle. Suddenly, Mom stopped the car. "This is it," she said.

Jason took one look. Then he ran, ran as if something inside him had been locked away too long. He ran across the hillside, through the trees, out back where a sagging old shed leaned against a large apple tree. He ran over slippery pine needles up the wooden steps to the veranda.

"It's pretty old," Mom said apologetically.

"Old! Oh, Mom!" Jason stretched out his hands, wishing he could say what he meant, but too many visions swept away the words. He had seen a bird's nest in the top branches of the oak. He had spotted tiny green apples on the apple tree. He had seen it all as it was now, as it would be for all the rest of the summer, the rest of the year, and years and years beyond that.

"The stairs creak," Mom said. "Some of the windows are stuck. And I'll have to do something about those awful kitchen cabinets. I think I'll paint the kitchen yellow. Look! Look at this view from the breakfast nook. I guess the roses will have to be trimmed back, and those vines..." She grinned at him. "Do you happen to know where I can find a good gardening book?"

Mom ran back and forth, laughing like a girl. Jason had never seen her so giddy. "I'll make all the curtains myself," she declared. "You and Dad can put up shelves. Did you see your room, the built-in chest under the window? I'll make you a cushion so you can sit there — it'll be like sitting in a tree house."

They stayed most of the day, roaming over the land, making plans, leaving only to go to the little town for lunch. Now, headed for home, Jason wondered whether he ought to wait for that Super-Duper fishing pole to come in at Matroni's. His old pole was split at the end. Maybe he'd buy a ten-dollar pole right away.

"I'm going to get a new fishing pole," he told Mom.

"Good idea," Mom said, nodding. "I guess you've got plenty of money saved up from weeding and working for Mr. Matroni."

"Hurry!" Jason cried suddenly. "Can't you drive any faster?"

"What's wrong? What's the rush?"

"I've got some things to do at home," Jason said. "I — I've got to mow the lawn."

His mother laughed.

"Hurry!" he repeated, frantic now for his money tree, which must be in desperate need of water. He'd tend to it the moment he got home.

But out front, playing baseball, was Dave Parker, and Jason couldn't resist shouting, "Dave! Guess what!"

Dave listened, bursting with questions, grasping Jason's sleeve to hold him there. "Tell me again — a pond? A shed for a clubhouse? Gee — that's great."

"You can come and spend a weekend with us after we move," Jason said, pulling away. "I've got to go now."

He would give the money tree an extra amount of water. Perhaps he could even squeeze out a few tears of happiness and add a vitamin pill.

With a shout, Dad came hurrying down the street from the bus stop. Excitedly, he told about the exam, while Mom, with equal excitement, told about their visit to the house. Suddenly, Mom whirled around nervously. "Where's Dinah? Good heavens, I left her in the house alone. Jason, go see what she's up to. Hurry!"

Jason ran inside and down the hall. Dinah was not in his parents' room or in the den. She was not in his room. But he saw telltale signs that she had been there. His bedspread was half pulled off. He could see that she had stood on the bed and...and...

With a cry he ran into the bathroom.

There stood Dinah, peering down into the churning toilet bowl. Seeing Jason, she clapped her hands and giggled. "Boat! Go bye-bye!"

"Dinah!" Jason screamed. "What did you do?"

He stared down into the swirling water. With a final slurping, sucking sound, Jason's fortune of ten-dollar bills went down, down, down.

That night Jason sat on his bed, still too stunned to feel any particular emotion. Spread out beside him were the ivory ball, the gold watch, and a single ten-dollar bill. Why Dinah had left that one on his dresser would always be a mystery. Why she so enjoyed watching things go flushing down the toilet was another. Maybe someday, when they were both much, much older, he would ask her. Maybe then he would even tell her that once she had gleefully flushed $260 down the toilet. But then, she would probably never believe him.

He would never tell a soul about the money tree. Because how could anybody be so irresponsible, so mixed-up, so downright stupid as to let a genuine real live money tree go dead and dry from lack of water?

Immediately after he had seen his savings go down the toilet, Jason had dashed out into the backyard. Thinking about it later, he told himself he had known all along what he would find. Still, the shock had been almost unbearable. The beautiful money tree had become a dry, brown, withered stalk. No amount of tears could revive it. No pleading, no magic incantations could bring it back to life. All the ten-dollar blossoms, which had hung so crisp and nearly ripe, looked like dead autumn leaves. They crumbled at his touch.

Jason had pulled out the dry stalk. To see it now, nobody would ever think it had been anything except a large weed.

Fiercely, Jason told himself that nobody, *nobody* would be so stupid as to forget to water a money tree. Unless...unless in a way he *wanted* to forget.

He heard Dad coming down the hall. Jason smiled wistfully to himself. There was nothing to hide anymore.

"Counting your treasures?" Dad asked.

Jason nodded. "I thought I'd buy a fishing pole with the ten dollars Grandpa left me," Jason said. "Do you think that would be all right?"

"I think," Dad replied, "that's exactly what Grandpa would have wanted you to do. He would have wanted you to take it and spend it on something you'd enjoy."

"I think so too," Jason agreed.

"I've got some fishing gear of my own put away," Dad said. "I used to go fishing a lot years ago."

"You did?" Jason had never seen his dad go fishing or golfing or anything like that. He had always been studying, at least for the past four years.

"Maybe I'll try my luck at that pond in Mill Valley," Dad said. "If you don't mind company."

"I don't mind company," Jason said. He felt that tightness in his throat again, but it dissolved and changed into a warm, wonderful feeling as Dad kissed him good night.

Jason got down under his covers, thinking about the money tree. He hadn't spent a single penny of it. Not on himself, anyway. He had given $170 to Mr. Matroni. It had made Mr. Matroni happy, and it had removed suspicion from him. But as Jason thought about it, he realized that something was still terribly wrong. One thing was unsettled, and it would remain that way forever.

Oh, no poltergeist could ever have planned a funnier, more mystifying prank! Jason began to grin to himself, nearly laughing aloud.

The United States of America now had $170 more than had been printed at the mint. Someday, somebody in Washington, D.C., would decide that all the money must be counted. Then it would be discovered that among all the millions and millions of dollars in the country, there was an extra $170.

What a commotion there would be! Again and again they would count the money with great adding machines and computers. The answer would always be the same — an extra $170. Who could explain it? At last some famous professor would frown helplessly and scratch his head and offer the only possible solution. A poltergeist. The poltergeist strikes again!

Jason laughed out loud, until his eyes were filled with laughing tears.

His door swung open. "Jason, what are you laughing about?" Mom whispered.

"Oh, nothing," he replied, giggling under his covers. "I'm just happy, I guess."